Philip De
Los Angeles 1971

Fire Sermon

Books by Wright Morris

Novels
FIRE SERMON
IN ORBIT
ONE DAY
CAUSE FOR WONDER
WHAT A WAY TO GO
CEREMONY IN LONE TREE
LOVE AMONG THE CANNIBALS
THE FIELD OF VISION
THE HUGE SEASON
THE DEEP SLEEP
THE WORKS OF LOVE
MAN AND BOY
THE WORLD IN THE ATTIC
THE MAN WHO WAS THERE
MY UNCLE DUDLEY

Photo-Text
GOD'S COUNTRY AND MY PEOPLE
THE HOME PLACE
THE INHABITANTS

Essays
A BILL OF RITES, A BILL OF WRONGS, A BILL OF GOODS
THE TERRITORY AHEAD

Anthology
WRIGHT MORRIS: A READER

FIRE
SERMON

Wright Morris

1817

HARPER & ROW, PUBLISHERS

NEW YORK, EVANSTON, SAN FRANCISCO,
LONDON

FIRST EDITION

STANDARD BOOK NUMBER: 06-013066-0

LIBRARY OF CONGRESS CATALOG CARD NUMBER: 73-156563

Book One

One

WHAT THE BOY SEES where the children are crossing makes his eyes squint. It is a long city block to the grade school exit where the old man gleams in the sun like a stop sign, and that is how he looks. He wears a yellow plastic helmet and an orange jacket with the word STOP stenciled on the back of it. The flaming color makes the word shimmer and hard to read. He might even be a dummy—the word GO is stenciled on the front of the helmet—but anyone who knows anything at all knows it's the boy's great-uncle Floyd. He's actually pretty much alive but those who don't know it cry out shrilly, "Are you a dummy, Mr. Warner?" When it's a boy who asks he better move fast, but if it's a girl the old man gives her a pat on the bottom with his Stop sign, just to hear her squeal.

One reason the boy likes to stand a long block away is that he doesn't want to be part of this horseplay. The squealing girls clap their hands, jump up and down, and shout some of the things they've heard the boys say. They don't mean it, not really, but the boy would just as soon not hear it, since he is known to all of them as the *old man's boy*. Actually, he is not the old man's boy, but it's hard to explain. Strictly speaking, he's an orphan, and the old man is just his next of kin. But the fact that he lives with him, and in a trailer, is more important than such an explanation. A further complication is that his name is Kermit Oelsligle. No one can explain how he happened to have such a strange name. When they ask him what his name is and he says Kermit, they say Kermit *what?* He no longer says *Oil-sleekle* at all, since it makes them laugh. My name's *Kurrr*-mit, he says, and only now, after more than a year, has the name stuck. His friend Manuel Gonzales says, "Hi, Kermit," and that's who he is. Everybody else, including his Uncle Floyd, calls him *boy*.

It's a five-minute walk, the way he loafs and dawdles, from where he stands on the corner to the schoolyard exit. Children are crossing. Some of the girls hold hands and skip. It is painful for a growing boy to watch a girl skip. Seen against the light of an October

afternoon their dresses are transparent and their legs
skinny. For weeks now two of them have cried

See you la-ter
Al-li-ga-tor

to the Uncle. They are sisters, and chant the same
thing when they leave the house in the morning. He
finds it no excuse that at five and six they are but
half his age.

The other thing he can't stand is the teakettle warble the Uncle makes blowing on his whistle. The
whistle has a "pea" in it, to give it the warble, but
only when blown with a strong blast. The Uncle no
longer has a strong blast, so the sound he makes is a
wet gurgling. The saliva in the whistle drips on his
front when it hangs by the thong from his neck. He
also wears it at meals. It drags in his egg when he
lowers his head to eat. The two eggs the Uncle eats
every morning account for his old age, his health, and
his "perk." He is eighty-two and has a lot of "perk"
for a man his age. If he eats only one egg in the morning he feels a loss of "perk" before lunch. The two
hard fried eggs, the slice of fried mush, the crumbs
and butter from his toast floating on his coffee, are
things the boy knows the way a bird knows its nest.
All that he knows often makes it impossible for him
to eat. He likes his egg not quite cooked so hard, but

the old man doesn't like him to eat a "live" chicken. That spot on the yolk is the eye of the chick, looking out. The Uncle no longer tells him to eat, insists that he eat, or even threatens him to eat, but merely slides the uneaten egg from the boy's plate to his own. Not being cooked as hard as it should be, it calls for more salt.

Neither of them like oatmeal, or eat it often, but it frequently comes up in their conversation. "A little oatmeal would stick to your ribs, boy," he says, since the boy always seems to be hungry. In spite of all he eats, he does almost next to nothing. At the boy's age (which is almost twelve) the Uncle got up at dawn, harnessed the horses, plowed forty acres of corn and alfalfa, fed and watered the team, then milked five cows and separated the cream before he sat down to supper. Thanks to a big bowl of oatmeal he was able to do that, although he preferred eggs.

Aside from food, the boy's big problem is waiting for the old man to finish his work. He is paid to stand at the crossing till the kiddie schoolyard is empty. Sometimes he has to go in and shoo the little ones out, like chickens. If one proves to be missing, he has a key to go and look in the schoolrooms. They hide in closets, or might be found sitting under desks. If the boy is around while this is going on someone will surely ask him what his name is, or why his name is so different from the old man's. If he is *not* around, where the Uncle can see him, the old man will shout to anybody he sees, wanting to know if they have seen that boy of *his*. It's just his way of talking, but talk like that has caused the boy a lot of trouble. He is related to the Uncle on his mother's side, and not especially close. Just a year ago, with his father, his mother, two four-month-old Hereford calves, and his dog, Schroeder, the boy was riding from their ranch, near Palmdale, to the State Fair in Sacramento. He never knew what happened. He and the dog had been sleeping in the back, and when he woke up it was all over. His mother, his father, his dog, and the two Herefords were dead. The boy wore a brace that kept his head from moving, and the nurse, Mrs. Seilers, had to feed him. She also read him the letters from his Aunt Viola, and replied that he would write to her when he could. His right arm itched day and night in a plaster cast.

If the boy had made a good adjustment to the fact that he was now an orphan, it was surely thanks to his Aunt Viola. She had carefully explained where his mother now was, waiting for him, and that she never for one moment stopped thinking of him. Here below, she had asked Aunt Viola to take her place. She sent the boy fudge, postcards of kittens and puppies, and a jigsaw puzzle that proved to be the face of the Saviour, a young man with a sad face and a pointed beard.

The boy's next of kin, and the person to take him, was of course his Aunt Viola, but she had been an invalid much of her life and needed a friendly neighbor to take care of her. Next in kin was his great-uncle, Floyd Warner, who also happened to be a lot nearer. He lived alone in a trailer, right beside a school the boy could go to. The Uncle came over to the hospital in a bus, because his own car was up on blocks in the trailer court, and it was not advisable to pump up the tires for such a short trip. The boy was brought down to the lobby by a nurse, where he saw this old man who looked like a cowhand. His coat was just the regular one to a suit, but the pants were tucked into the tops of his half boots. He wore a two-gallon hat. Kermit had seen old geezers like him on the TV serials, but considered him too old to be his next of kin. "God-a-mighty, boy," he said, "don't you know who I am?" The boy didn't, but he said, "You're Uncle Floyd?" "Seems I am, boy," he replied. "Where your duds?"

The boy had very few duds he hadn't managed, just lying in bed, to grow out of. What he hadn't grown out of, he had on. His mother's things had been sent in a trunk to Aunt Viola, and what the boy could still wear he had in a duffel. The old man used it as a pillow to rest his head on during the bus ride back. He was not much of a talker. When they got to where they stopped he said, "Here's where we get off." The boy didn't *dis*like the Uncle, understand, he simply didn't want it known he was his *next* of kin. Especially when he wore the hard hat that made him look like some sort of bug.

From the backside, which is how the boy usually sees him, he looks even sillier than from the front, since a face has been painted on the hard hat to fool people into thinking he is looking toward them. The face wears goggles and a big friendly smile. If his back is turned, the people in cars might not hear his toot on the whistle. There is no longer much difference between his long blast and his short. He lacks the wind. The boy has tried it himself, and the fault may be that the pea in the whistle, which is made of wood, is so wet and heavy with saliva blowing on it doesn't do much. The warble is like that of bird ornaments on Christmas trees.

At the schoolyard gate the boy steps inside and slurps water at the fountain, forcing a thin stream of it through the slit between his front teeth. That is something new: he owes it to the accident. "Just don't you forget," his mother liked to tell him, "every dark cloud has a silver lining."

A small boy with a bandaged eye stands at the curb waiting to cross. He has already crossed the street four or five times. He thinks it's a game. The Uncle says,

"Run along home, kid," and gives him a strong nudge with his Stop sign. He does not like kids. He thinks they are all a pain in the ass. The fact that he has never had kids of his own he thinks the greatest blessing of his life. They grow up to be hippies, criminals, drug addicts, sex maniacs, or basketball players. The boy should be grateful he is too short to be a basketball player.

The Uncle notes he is there, and goes along the fence to a large wooden box at one end of the schoolhouse. The box contains playground equipment for the kiddies, and the sloping lid is padlocked. The Uncle's keys are on a chain attached to his belt. One key is for the padlock, one key is for the school (if a child is missing, that is the first place to look), one key is for the car, now up on blocks, one key is for the trailer, and four or five keys no longer serve any purpose. One is to the car he traded in on the trailer, and one is to a garage he rented in Ojai, where he kept the trailer while he had his prostate operation, which he paid for in cash. The other keys must have once fit something. and there is always a chance they might fit something again. No one with the sense they were born with ever throws away a key. He raises the lid of the box and puts in the Stop sign, his yellow hard hat, and then the orange jacket, folding the jacket so it won't crack along one of the seams. From the box he takes a cap, tan in color, with the earflaps up, tied in a bow at the crown, and a folded shopping bag in which he will carry the laundry. He puts the cap on his head, and when he turns to face the boy he looks like Bugs Bunny. Other old men the boy knows either go without hats, or wear something that hides what they should be ashamed of, but his Uncle Floyd looks like either a bug or something worse. This couldn't always have been so, since his Aunt Viola, who would rather die than say something untruthful, often took a full page in one of her letters to say how the girls had carried on about him. "Dear Boy"—she would write (these were really Kermit's letters)— "there were broken hearts all over Humboldt County when he married Estelle." The boy had to accept that on faith, and he did, since Viola had faith enough to save half the people in hell. That was the sober opinion of a man with no faith whatsoever, Floyd Warner. Now he walked toward the boy pulling on the sweater his sister Viola had sent him for Christmas, the sleeves so long he had to roll the cuffs up. The cook in the Acme diner said he looked like Popeye the sailor. The boy could believe it, although he had no idea how Popeye looked. Sometimes the boy lagged behind, to give the impression they were just walking along, but not together, or he might walk a step or two ahead as if he needed more room to play with his yo-yo, which he often did. The Uncle said, "Think you'll ever learn to work it?"

After fourteen months the boy understood this was just his way of talking. He did not talk just to hear himself talk, or spoil you with praise. "You hatching that egg?" he would say, when the boy fried one, or "You waiting for hell to freeze over?" He was full of expressions that made no sense whatsoever. How did hell freeze over? It was something *he* might have heard as a boy. Kermit had never seen anything frozen over larger than a milk can or a feed trough, although he understood everything froze up back on the plains. His Uncle and his mother both came from there, and his great-aunt Viola still lived back there. His father was from Texas, which he often said was cold as a witch's tit.

Most of the people in Rubio knew the Uncle as the crossing guard to the grade school corner. They said "Hi there!" to him, when they saw him on the street, and the children cried "Hello, Mr. Warner!" There was nothing to gain in being unfriendly with a crossing guard.

The boy lagging, they go along Alameda, the sidewalk steaming with the city sprinklers. In the Uncle's opinion, the hippies in Rubio would never wash their feet if it wasn't for the sprinklers. They walk in the wet grass in the street divider, leaving the tracks of their feet as far north as Tracy. At Tracy and Alameda there is a movie, a drugstore, and shops for people who carry their groceries. If they shop every day but Sunday there is a very little for the boy to carry. They eat a lot of potatoes. Neither of them understand where all the margarine seems to go. In the hot weather, as it is in October, in order to help keep the trailer cool, they cook less and eat a lot of frozen meat pies. They come in four flavors, beef, chicken, turkey, and tuna, which they heat up in a small electric oven. Another thing the Uncle can't account for is where all the milk goes. The boy can. He drinks two glasses for lunch, then he has two more after lunch while the Uncle is busy at the traffic corner. He likes his own milk straight from the carton just before he goes to bed to settle his stomach, the night air in the trailer cooled by the draft from the refrigerator door. The boy would like to have ice cubes made from grape Kool-Aid, but the ice compartment is used to store frozen berries and meat pies. The boy likes the berries while they are half frozen, and may have already ruined his stomach. The Uncle likes them on his cereal, or in a tall glass covered with canned milk.

The boy's yo-yo casts a shadow on the wall of the school like a ball he was trying to throw away and couldn't. In this part of the walk he lags far behind, stopping in one place so he can watch the shadow. His own shadow is six feet tall, or almost. Not much can be said about how he looks except for the flap of hair on his forehead. It is always there, like a tilted awning, and explains the birdlike cock of his head. If he had real long hair, like the Beatles, he would wipe it back and it would stay there, but the sides and back of his head are clipped. "Goddam it to hell, you want to look like a hippie?" He didn't know. It would take some pondering. He couldn't bear the shame of somebody taking him for a girl. Nor did he want his mother turning in her grave (as the old man said she certainly would), since Aunt Viola had written how she was buried with her father, her mother, and her mother's mother, in a plot so small there had not been room for *his* father, or a marker of her own. In a way he hadn't noticed while she was alive he was now aware of his mother's presence. "Dear Boy," Aunt Viola wrote him, "your mother's loving eyes are always upon you—" Even allowing for her having other interests that could be a lot. He thought of her as younger than he remembered because she had been "a little girl" to Viola, who had last seen her three years before she was married.

The Uncle is not concerned that the boy lags behind, or is held up by the light at Alameda and Shoreline. He didn't especially like kids, and in his eighty-first year this ten-year-old boy had moved into his trailer. It was not the boy's fault he had no nearer relations, nor that Floyd Warner didn't care much for his mother. It was her child, one year behind in his schooling, thanks to the way they moved around when they cared to, that he now saw stringing beads when he opened his eyes in the morning. Did people send a boy to school to learn to string beads? If the Uncle had five more years of life, which was two more than his own father, this boy would still be a kid in the Rubio high school playing with his yo-yo and stringing beads. The trailer would be full of his hippie friends, all smoking pot.

The Uncle's anger was divided, and weakened, by his worry about what might happen to the boy, and his rage against the pack of mongrels that would soon take over his trailer. It had been his home for twenty-seven years. No trailer in the camp was as neat and clean. No teen-age boy could be expected to learn how to use the stove, how to change the gas, how to save the lights, and how to get rid of ants. An old fool and his wife (the Uncle will *not* stop thinking in such terms) who live in an apartment facing the trailer court have been waiting eight years for Warner to die, and to buy his trailer. He has heard from Mrs. Leidy, the court owner, that the woman is making curtains for it. Just to think about them renews the Uncle's lease on life. But renewal or no, he will not live forever and one day they (both still in their sixties) will make the boy an offer and move in with their three cats.

If the boy is underfoot, the Uncle is seldom easy of mind. If he lags behind, or is held up at a light, he might lose him for five or ten minutes, there being one drugstore and two markets he will have to check. The old man has a deal with Mr. Brundage, of Self-Serv, that if he spends as much as five dollars he can take the cart along and let the boy bring it back, Mr. Brundage knowing that Floyd Warner is as good as his word. With that in mind he will pick up their laundry, fluffed and folded (you can't do laundry for a boy in a trailer), and a ten-pound sack of charcoal briquets, on sale at Varney's outlet. The Rubio Laundrolette is full of new washers, a new gas fluff and drier, a play-pen for babies, and a machine that will give the old man four quarters for a dollar. He has used it three times, and it makes no mistakes. The Laundrolette attendant is a girl in her second year at the Rubio high school. She has five lower teeth, no upper teeth, and a child fifteen months old. These simple facts are on display six days a week, but the old man can't believe them. He accepts them: believe them he cannot. At eighty-two he has all but two of his own teeth (impacted molars pulled in Kansas City) and to actually see this toothless girl, with her child, is no help at all in helping him to believe it. He thought her one of these Okie women who came out in the thirties and forties. Her color is sallow, free of makeup, and her public expression is that of a seamstress with a row of straight pins between her lips. This habit was formed when her teeth hurt her, and without her teeth she still has it. It was not something she learned to conceal the few she still has. They are bunched all at the front, like the teeth of prairie dogs poisoned by grain, or hit by something, lying sprawled on their backs with their feet in the air, their mouths open. The old man had seen thousands of them in his day, and he knows how they look. Under the sacklike dress of an oatmeal color her breasts hang loose and get in her way when she is folding clothes. Out of a lifetime of habit Floyd War-ner asks a person his or her name, the first time he meets him, but he cannot bring himself to speak to this girl. Would he rather she *didn't* have a name? Yes, he would rather that. She has displayed no interest in his and lets him find his own bundle, when he calls for it, while she goes on folding clothes, or nursing her baby. That too is something the old man has seen when he let a sow litter in the warmth of the kitchen, sitting up all night to keep her from rolling on her own brood. She goes to school: he has seen her seated on one of the idle teeter-totters, in the playground, and as much as he detests the idle gossip of women he is curious about the child's father. What possessed him? His puzzlement is greater than his disgust. The girl's infant (they all looked alike to Floyd Warner) often occupied the hamper that sat on the scales for weighing clothes. It did not disturb the mother if a nearsighted customer dumped her bundle of laundry over him, her, or whatever it was.

Shoreline Avenue in Rubio is lined with palms and parking meters. The palms are now so high that only people traveling south on the freeway see their tops, said to be the hideout of a new breed of tree-climbing rats. This rumor persists because the fire department has no extension ladder that will reach to their tops. The west end of Shoreline is Rubio Beach, once a sedate, almost exclusive promenade and bathing center, now the site of a swarming hippie love-in during the spring of the year. They come straggling along the streets, singly and in clusters, thousands of them, some love-ining as they go, like the strayed and lost remnants of some deranged but irresistible Pied Piper. Colonel Gertler, who served on the Western Front, compares it to the flow of refugees from the east. Many of them were children. They too wore the stoned vacant expressions, but carried no flowers. During this invasion the older residents attempt to confine the younger ones to their playrooms. Beach fires light the sky. There is frequently a rumbling noise that compares to that from the freeway. The old man and the boy watch it all from the safety of the trailer court, where the gate is locked, seated on two armless camp chairs at the door of the trailer. This 4 × 5 spot, a mini-verandah, is filled in with green gravel, to give a grassy effect, and is sheltered above by a metal awning with alternate bands of yellow and white. There is room to one side for the barbecue grill, on which they do most of their summer cooking, charburgers being the old man's specialty.

FRESH HORSE MEAT DAILY is still visible on the window of Augie's Pet Emporium, but it was not sold only as pet food when Floyd Warner settled in Rubio. He had tried it himself. Few things disturb him so much as his squeamishness in this matter. He liked horses no better than cows. He thought them as dumb. But along about his third juicy bite of mustang filet, the best cut, he had to push his plate away and settle for a strong cup of black coffee. It was one of many things he had not mentioned to the boy. With several other kids he was inside the pet store trying to get the myna bird to say f—— Nixon. Floyd Warner doubted he ever really said it, but that was the story, and it made good business. The old man did not use such words himself, but he had always been free with most of the others. The name of the Lord or his earthly son figured prominently in these outbursts, since the old man considered religion—all religions—the scandal of the century. The long and fluent relief of cursing was still one of his respected talents. Bigger and tougher men had stood slack-jawed to listen to him. This strain of rage in him revealed itself in various abuses: the beating of horses, the breaking of tools, the frightening of children, and fancy cursing. His sister, Viola, had written to the boy, "No one curses so elegantly as dear Floyd," which both pleased and distressed him, since he had not known he had cursed before *her*. But more than likely he had, their father being the first great hate of his life.

"Come along, boy," he said, and they go along together to where dogs blocked the entrance of the Self-Serv market. Five dogs, two of them the size of yearling calves. The way things were going he would not be surprised if they one day turned and just gobbled him up, but they probably wouldn't because they had it softer the way it was. Like people, they were now too smart for their own good.

The boy tried three carts before he found one without a flat wheel. Another thing he didn't like were front wheels that wobbled, or one wheel that stuck when he made a turn. Cart wheels were damaged by old men, or old ladies, who sneaked off with them without asking permission, and bounced them off curbs, or ran them over bricks, or kept them at home for children to play with. (There were two market carts right at this instant being used as playpens in camp trailers.) Today the old man buys a sack of white potatoes, a sack of red potatoes, two bunches of carrots, two cucumbers, two half gallons of milk, two dozen brown eggs (white eggs had yolks so pale he could hardly see them), two pounds of margarine, one jar of peanut butter, one jar of strawberry jam, three loaves of sourdough bread, five one-pound packages of ground chuck, three pounds of chicken wings, one pound of legs, and the leg and thigh of a tom turkey, big as a dog's. At the checkout counter they buy two packages of gum, and one plastic bag of Hershey kisses. They both watch each item as the cashier, Miss Tomlin, rings it up. The young man who puts it in the brown bags is Skip Fletcher, a basketball star at Rubio High School. The boy is afraid to look for his face in the big muff of hair. The old man says, "Put all of that in three bags, will you, boy?" Kermit has been waiting for him to say that, and now that it is said he takes a grip on the cart. The old man holds up the line to open the sack of Hershey kisses, fish one out, and fumble with the foil wrapper. He pops it into his mouth and moves toward the door. In no way whatsoever does he show the faintest inkling that he has just escaped with his life. Skip Fletcher doesn't show it either, stuffing his hand into a bag, but everybody else in the market knows it, and just waits for Floyd Warner to drop dead. The boy is so sure that one day he will—if first Skip Fletcher doesn't kill him—that he has a little speech he plans to give when they ask him what in the world happened. This speech will explain, as most Rubio people know, that the old man calls people "boy" if they are younger than he is, which includes all but four or five people in the county. He says "boy" like other people say "Hi." He doesn't mean one thing or another by it, he likes white boys just as little as black boys, and possibly even less than people in general. If this speech will not make him popular it will nevertheless explain that although he might be peculiar, he is not what you would call a racist, or anything like that.

Nothing happens, however, and they go through the doors that open with a swish, and keep the dogs out. They stop next door for the bag of briquets stacked in the wheelbarrow in front of the hardware. Mr. Muzzey, who owns it, looks as old as Uncle Floyd but he says "Hi there, you kids," and makes change from his own pocket. The old man does not like this "kid" stuff, but he considers Mr. Muzzey so old and senile he has to be excused. It is people like Muzzey he refers to when he speaks of "old farts," which is quite often, as distinct from "oldsters," in which group he considers himself.

Now the boy takes the cart, and they go east toward the barren embankment of the freeway, the guard rail at the top level with the blur of passing cars. At this hour of the day it is picking up. Traffic from San Jose is streaming north, and traffic from as far as San Francisco—where the boy has not been— is roaring to the south. This sound is now so consistent they don't actually hear it. It is a wind-noise, or a sea-sound, to which he has grown accustomed. In the morning, early, he is aware of its diminished roar and thinks of that as morning—just as now, and on through the twilight, he will think of this noise as evening. There is seldom no sound, even late at night. In moments of silence his Uncle Floyd will jerk in his bunk, and pop his head up. Sometimes he will say aloud, "What the hell was that?" When he was inexperienced, early in the winter, the boy would say, "Nothing, Uncle Floyd," but in time he learned this was worse than if he pretended sleep and said nothing. How could it be *nothing?* It had to be *something* that woke him up. He would lean on his elbow, listening, until he caught the whine of an approaching car, and by the time it had come up and passed he might be back asleep.

The main entrance to the trailer court is two blocks

east, at the exit to the freeway, but in three years it has been seldom used because most of the guests are on a permanent basis. It is now a camp, more than a court, and the sign on the freeway had been changed to say so, but people who were new or just plain dumb sometimes pulled off and were disappointed. They were often people traveling late at night, having come up from L.A., or come down from Portland, and the lights of their cars, stopped at the entrance, always made the boy think of accidents and police cars. They shone directly on the Warner trailer and lit up the inside like a bolt of lightning. His Uncle would have to get up, pull on his pants, and go out in his bare feet to speak to the people, then try and help them get turned around so they could get back on the freeway. These were the times his Uncle might curse from the time he got up till he came back to the trailer. The boy did not understand what his Aunt Viola meant by elegant. He was not shocked by cursing since he had been raised among cowhands, who like to curse at horses and cattle, but none of them went on and on half so long, or cursed as if they really meant it. His Uncle Floyd, with his head in the lights as if a police car spotlight had caught him, would talk a stream without any letup, his head pumping like a dog barking, his face so red it made his hair look white. He used a few words the boy had never heard, but he never used the words the boy heard the most. These were the "dirty" words kids wrote on buildings and on the walls and doors of lavatories. He couldn't help but know those words, but he was never so furious he used one. No, not once. Twenty yards down the street, where they could see it and turn, hung a NO VACANCY sign with the NO on a blinker, but either they thought it was out of order, or didn't see it, or were just ornery, since they would drive right by it and then honk at the chain. This chain was taken down and a high fence put up after what was known as the "incident." "We don't want an incident like that again," Mrs. Leidy had said, and the fence had stopped them. Anyone could walk around it, on either side, but no one with any sense would try and drive through it.

The boy recalled the incident very well. It had rained all day and Uncle Floyd had gone to bed even earlier than usual, leaving his boots and his lantern-sized flashlight where he could reach them if something flooded. If a wind came up and blew down a lot of leaves the three drains in the camp would clog up in a jiffy, and there was nothing to do but straddle one and rake off the leaves by the handful. The boy held the lamp, wearing a poncho-type raincape that dragged on the ground.

He slept right through the noise they must have

made coming in. That was unusual in itself, since Volkswagen motors, especially the old ones, make quite a racket. Someone had got out and let down the chain, then they had pulled right over it into the camp, parking under an oak. When the boy did wake up the old man was pulling on his boots, and cursing. It wasn't raining so hard, just a light drizzle, but a film of water glistened over the bricks in the drive. Out there in the dark, where he couldn't see a thing, there were yelps and shrieks like you hear in a dog pound, some of them worse. The boy couldn't see a thing until the old man had clapped on his rain hat and stepped outside, switching on his light. About twenty yards away, directly in the beam, what the boy saw looked like a jungle movie. They had a broadside view of the Volkswagen bus and it was painted every color of the rainbow, but most of it green, red, and yellow, like flowering plants. The windows were curtained, and like something he saw through a screen of foliage. No lights. Just the crazy yelping and hooting. The Uncle kept his light trained on the cab and when he got up beside it he banged on the door. Nobody answered. There was too much racket for them to hear. The Uncle set the lantern on the ground and using both hands he tried to get the door open, and gave it several kicks. The noises eased up and the old man yelled, "What in the God-a-mighty hell are you up to?"

"We're havin' an orgy!" came the reply. "What the hell you think?"

The boy heard that as plainly as if he had said it himself. The old man was so flabbergasted he just stood there, holding the light. The yelping started again, and the boy would swear he saw the bus rock. The old man went back and tried the rear door, then he picked up a brick that marked the edge of the drive, gripped it with both hands, and slammed it against the side of the bus. The noise of it made the boy wince, and close his eyes. He did that maybe four, five, six times, each time a little harder than the previous, when the rear door of the car swung wide, with a bang, and a long-haired girl leaped into the drive. She was absolutely naked except for her streaming hair. Another girl followed her, then a boy (he could see well enough to tell the boys, all right), then a girl swinging what might have been a dress, then two boys in shirts but without their pants, their stiff peckers looking like horns as they ran into the dark. Another boy followed, dragging a girl along with him, then he let go of her hand and took off by himself, leaving her to wheel around, like she was dizzy, then stumble off in the same direction. The last one leaped out with an armful of blankets, tripped on a trailing corner, and sprawled on his face. The boy would not soon forget his naked straddle-legged stance as he scooped things up. How many were there? It would be hard to be sure. The boy felt they would keep coming, like the next fireball out of a Roman candle. But it stopped, and behind the soft drizzle he could hear sounds like deer scrambling through brush, or a pack of hounds. None of them ever came back. They left the car to sit right where it was so everyone in camp looked it over in the morning. There was not much in it but piles of old bedding, several pairs of blue jeans, and maybe two dozen girls' panties, some of them left over—in the Sheriff's opinion—from orgies somewhere else. There was also marijuana in the dashboard ash-tray and two gallon-size jugs of Mountain Red wine, one about half full, but nothing at all to indicate whose car it was, or who *they* were. The Oregon license had been swiped from another car. Until this incident occurred nobody had known that where the camp now stood was once known as the "jungle," and was used by high school boys and girls who parked there to neck. These looked like young hippies, they couldn't have been that old, but they must have smelled it out or heard about it somewhere, since they all ran off and disappeared as if they knew their way around. When he spoke about it to Mrs. Leidy, Uncle

Floyd referred to them as "young heathens," and a striking example of what the world was coming to.

Floyd Warner's arrangement with Mrs. Leidy—he did not consider himself in her "employ"—paid him sixty dollars a month plus free trailer parking. For his part he raked the gravel walks, watered the plants, and kept an eye on the place. Some years back Mrs. Leidy had felt that Floyd Warner might have filled in well for Major Leidy, but when he turned up with a boy who had no other close kin her manner had grown cooler. Since Major Leidy's death she ate mostly nuts she cracked herself, and no meat. "The energy you use digesting meat," she told the boy, "you could convert to a higher consciousness." The boy replied that he ate it because he was hungry and liked the taste. In the old days Floyd Warner often set up her grill, knowing how to get the most out of the charcoal, and if he didn't stay for supper, having food of his own, he would drop around later to watch "Gunsmoke" with her on the TV. Her trailer had a living room almost twenty feet wide and watching TV in it did not give the Uncle headaches. All of that had stopped, and perhaps just as well, or the boy might have become one of those TV addicts, with nothing but "TV snow" on his mind.

Two

THERE ARE TWENTY-SIX TRAILERS in Live Oak Camp, plus eleven dogs, nine cats, and four children, not counting Kermit Oelsligle. Dogs are not allowed to roam, and when walked on a leash have to make their mess off the gravel paths. Live Oak Camp is modest, by most standards, having no swimming pool, public showers, view of the sea, or cable TV, but it does offer shade, reasonable rates, and walking distance to schools and shopping. Nineteen of the twenty-six trailers have been here for at least ten years. That also pretty well dates them—and the people you will find in them. When they settled for a trailer good rentals were scarce, and they considered the move temporary, something to live in while they took time to look around. In less than half the time most of them took land prices doubled, and the dollar dwindled—which happens to be why, they tell the boy, they are where they are. A boy his age could hardly care less, but he is new to the camp, old enough to talk to, and brought up to say "Yes, ma'am," when asked to do something. He has also been nowhere, knows very little, and therefore should find the stories of old men of interest. Most of these stories begin, "You wouldn't believe it, my boy—" and most of the time they are right.

The trailers sit in three rows, in a herringbone pattern, each row divided by a narrow strip of blacktop. The boy considers blacktop the best surface of all for roller skates and food carts. The noise is reduced, but not so much the dogs don't start barking when they pass by. Mrs. Leidy's Welsh corgi does not like the boy, and claws at the metal screen door to her trailer, although all the boy did was catch him peeing on one of their own trailer wheels, and gave a bang on the wall. The corgi had kicked gravel all over the place as he took off.

"You go along, boy," the old man tells him, and turns off at the entrance to Mrs. Leidy's. She has a flagstone walk leading to her door, with a picket fence around her rock garden. The day's incoming mail will be in the birdbox sheltered by her patio awning. One of the Uncle's chores is to deliver the mail. On the average it takes him half an hour or more if he gets into a discussion. The older trailer residents (fifteen years or more) feel the younger residents are noisy and irresponsible. They don't talk to each other. There have been two unverified cases of dog poisoning. The younger residents don't speak to anybody, but the older ones talk to Floyd Warner with the idea that he will speak to Mrs. Leidy. Her point of view is, if anybody doesn't like it, they can move. Floyd Warner has made few complaints himself, but he has made so many for others Mrs. Leidy may feel he identifies with them, and when she says *if anybody doesn't like it, they can move*, it's very clear that she means *anybody*. Move where? She knows very well he hasn't so much as had air in his tires for years.

Because he gets his rent free, the old man's trailer is separate from the rest, under the oak at the entrance. It takes up less room. The boy likes the trailer sitting where it is, since it is more like they were off somewhere, camping. The Uncle's car is under an olive green tarpaulin. Both the car and the trailer are up on blocks (with boxes of ivy cuttings under the trailer), but you would never believe the trailer dated from the thirties if it wasn't for the model A wheels. The man who built it, then living in Arizona, must have gone on to make his fortune somewhere, since this trailer looked ahead to the bullet-type aluminum numbers in the fifties. All the joints in the shell were hand welded, and the only leaks, in all those years, were at the windows. He had even thought of screens, on the inside, and a water system you could attach to a garden hose. It suited the Uncle fine, but it proved to be small for a man and a boy. Only one person could move around at a time, so one had to stay in bed, or go for a walk somewhere. The boy's bunk was an upper, put in by his Uncle, but it was twelve inches shorter and eight inches narrower than the bunk bed below it. A crib mattress was just the right length, but not so thick he couldn't feel the ropes that held it. When an acorn from the oak fell on the metal roof he jumped a foot. All winter long it pinged like a helmet when it rained. His only serious complaint was that the old man, all winter long, got up before daylight to cook breakfast, which they would eat by the hissing glow of his camp lantern. It seemed hours would pass before the boy went to school. In the empty playground he would swing on the swings, balance the teeter-totters, play with his yo-yo, and be so hungry he was almost starved by the time the bell rang. He was able to stay alive by eating the Fig Newtons his Uncle believed kept them both healthy and regular. If your bowels don't move, he said, you just help yourself. The boy did just that, scooting back to the trailer for a handful of them at recess, and gulping down milk if the Uncle was off somewhere. Floyd Warner was accustomed to a big dinner, having been up for six or seven hours, after which he took off his shoes and took a nap. If he was still asleep at the afternoon recess the boy would make himself a peanut butter sandwich, gulp some more milk, and grab a few Fig Newtons on his way out. It sometimes seemed that the more he ate, the hungrier he got. Coming back with the groceries, he had to be careful not to go hog wild and make himself sick, or eat so much he lost his appetite for supper. If he couldn't eat, the old man knew he was sick. His cure for sickness was not to eat anything at all, and starve into submission whatever it was that was troubling you, or take three tablespoonfuls of castor oil and wash it out. The boy had learned to leave nothing but grease streaks on his plate.

On a day like this one they would barbecue chuckburgers on the new grill. Floyd Warner did not believe in Blue Chip stamps, nor would he patronize a store that promoted such hooey, but a woman whose child used the school crossing had one day just given him all these stamps. It had been the boy's chore to lick them and put them in the books. Rather than risk losing them all in the mail, the Uncle rode the bus with them to San Jose, where he went to the store, exchanged them for the grill, and returned home. A metal hood protected food from the wind, and there was a crank to turn roasting chickens. The boy took charge of the grill, and prepared the fire. He had reduced to eight the number of briquets necessary to charbroil four chuckburgers, leaving heat enough to percolate the coffee. With the hamburgers they ate strips of fresh cucumber, sprinkled with garlic salt.

A privet hedge a block long and almost eight feet high screens the trailer camp from the school. Floyd Warner had planted that hedge himself and saw to it that it was clipped and watered. He did this after supper, when the boy could help him, since it required moving the hoses from nozzle to nozzle. The stooping and pulling was something the boy was young and strong enough to do. By the time they had reached the end of the hedge, on Shoreline, it was time to start all over again. Some trailer residents complained that the flowering privet gave them hay fever and sinus headaches, but Mrs. Leidy believed that all such disturbances were in the mind. She liked the sweet smell of the privet herself, and if people didn't like it they didn't have to breathe it. Floyd Warner liked it. It reminded him of a lilac bush that bloomed on one side of the porch when he was a boy, filling a house he otherwise hated with its almost sickening fragrance. He had a very good nose. Viola used to say he could see through his nose. The boy did not understand why anyone should hate a house, or even find the smell of flowers so sweet they were sickening, but he listened to this story with his eyes wide since it was the first that the old man had told him. He had thought, when he arrived, that his great-uncle Floyd would be like his father's uncle, Harvey Stambaugh, who began to talk once he had swallowed his food, and went on talking till he had once more filled up his mouth. He had some remarkable stories to tell, but the boy had already forgotten most of them. His Uncle Floyd said next to nothing, day in and day out. He usually talked only when he gave orders, which he had been accustomed to do as a farmer with as many as fifteen hired hands during threshing time. The boy would have liked to have heard more of that, but there he stopped. The only time he did more than give orders was when he read to the boy from his books or read him Aunt Viola's weekly letter. These letters were addressed to Kermit Oelsligle, not to Floyd Warner, and the boy could have read them very well for himself, but either his Uncle didn't believe he *could* read, or he liked to get and read letters. Aunt Viola seemed to know this, as she would say, "and now, Floyd, you old rascal—" and say something that was meant personally for him. Floyd was five years younger than Viola, and she had always been his favorite sister. How his sister could have lived for eighty-seven long years and still believe the foolish nonsense their father had taught them was something that Floyd Warner could not understand. He would put the letter face down in his lap, and put a hand to his eyes. The boy did not understand what this "nonsense" was except that it had to do with religion, living forever in heaven, where she would rejoin all those who had died. It did seem a little farfetched, but the boy didn't know much about it. There was a God, of course, but he was vague on the details. His Uncle Floyd had given his life to this study, and expressed himself very strongly. "You can tell her she'll have to do without me!" he shouted. "I'd rather burn in hell than be with that old bastard!" That old bastard was *their* father, so the boy knew better than ever write and tell her. But the Uncle had also told her that, time after time, when he wrote in the past. "Don't let that old scalawag tell you his stories," she wrote Kermit. "There's so much the Good Lord has to forgive him already!" But she wasn't really worried. The boy knew she felt it would all turn out all right. The Lord knew everything, and one thing He knew was that Floyd Warner was a true and a good man, one who belonged in heaven, in spite of the foolish things he said. The boy agreed with that. If good and true men were in heaven, that was where he would be.

Two or three times a month he might read to the boy from Colonel Ingersoll's *Forty-Four Complete Lectures*, a volume with a faded red binding and

Colonel Ingersoll's picture on the cover. The type was in two columns, and most of it so small Uncle Floyd took his glasses from his nose and used one lens like a magnifier, reading with his head tipped to one side.

There never has been a man or woman of genius from the southern hemisphere [What was that? the boy wondered] because the Lord didn't allow the right climate to fall upon the land. It falls upon the water. There never was much civilization except where there has been snow, and an ordinarily decent winter. [Uncle Floyd had it in his youth, so he no longer needs it.] You can't have civilization without it. Where man needs no bedclothes but clouds, revolution is the normal condition of such a people. It is the winter that gives us a home; it is the winter that gives us a fireside, and the family relation, and all the beautiful flowers of love that adorn that relation. Civilization, liberty, justice, charity and intellectual advancement are all flowers that bloom in the drifted snow.

The boy had never set his eyes upon drifted snow except on the TV or in the movies. He planned to buy a snowmobile one of these days and test the theory out. A favorite passage he had heard many times had to do with the making of Adam and Eve.

After the sleep had fallen on this man the Supreme Being took a rib, or, as the French would call it, a cutlet, out of him, and from that he made a woman; and I am willing to swear, taking into account the amount and quality of the raw material used, this was the most magnificent job ever accomplished in this world. (Uproarious

*laughter from his listeners.) Well, after he got the woman
done she was brought to the man, not to see how she
liked him but to see how he liked her. He liked her, and
they started housekeeping—*

Uncle Floyd found all of this so funny he would
have to stop reading and sit muttering curses. "Jump-
ing Jehoshaphat!" he would say, "O Jesus save me!"
along with remarks the boy censored. He might just
sit with his head in his hands and forget where it was
he had broken off reading. "Where was I, boy?" he
would ask, his eyes shiny with laugh tears, and the boy
often wondered. He did understand that Colonel Ingersoll had him doing the two things he liked to do
most, laugh and curse. Next came dominoes, which
was something he could do with the boy. The boy
liked to play games, especially checkers, but not with
someone who took the game so seriously. The Uncle
kept his finger on the piece till he had figured all the
moves and made himself almost dizzy trying to peer
around it. If he overlooked something it made him so
furious he would curse, and blame it on his eyes.
"Goddam it to hell, boy, I must be color-blind!" The
Uncle liked to win, but he wouldn't cheat. The boy
liked to cheat. "Is that a cockroach, Uncle Floyd?"
he would ask, and stare into the corner behind him.
When the old man turned to look he would give himself a checker, or take one off. Thinking about cock-

roaches also took his mind off the game. The boy paid for all of this when his Uncle read to him from *When a Man's a Man*, by Harold Bell Wright. The book had been given to him by Aunt Viola, with her name at the front.

There is a land where a man, to live, must be a man. . . . In this land every man is—by divine right—his own king; he is his own jury, his own counsel, his own judge, and— if it must be—his own executioner.

Hearing that the boy felt what he knew must be guilt, and knew himself to be a lesser man than the Uncle. On the other hand, with his Aunt Viola's help, he might improve himself. In the same breath the Uncle described her as a silly child and a saintly woman, a portrait the boy accepted as true to her remarkable nature. Until she wrote to him he had never received a letter, or known that all letters were once hand-written. She still wrote a "fine Spencerian hand," but recently it had become a little shaky. The boy felt he had come to know her pretty well—the big house she lived in, the two cats she lived with, and the presence of the Lord in all of her thoughts. Aunt Viola's picture of Uncle Floyd was perhaps even stranger than his picture of her. Her letters always ended with the question "How is that wicked old scalawag you live with?" Uncle Floyd *wicked?* What in the world was a scalawag? When he read that

Uncle Floyd would take off his glasses and rub at his eyes with his knuckles. The boy was dying to know, but feared to ask him what a scalawag was. He would also just as soon read his own letters—they all began, *My dearest boy*—but he considered the old man a better reader of her Spencerian hand. First he would hold the letter to the lamp, to see which end was the best one to open, in case it had clippings inside. He never failed, after he took out the letter, to shake the envelope to make sure it was empty.

Aunt Viola's weekly letters were often read several times because the first time might get the Uncle so aggravated he found it hard to go on. Not all of Viola's letters were in that vein, but at her age her old friends were dying, and she felt the need to reassure Floyd that he would see them all again, and they would see him. "Only if they all burn in hell!" he had shouted, and thrown that letter on the floor as if he meant to stomp on it. He didn't, of course. He put it with the others in his locked metal file. They were the *boy's* letters, addressed to him, personally, but all he wanted to do was make sure he wouldn't lose them, and have them to read when he got a little older and had some sense.

Aunt Viola wrote the letters to "her" boy on Sunday, and unless something went wrong they were received on Tuesday, and nothing had gone wrong. His

Uncle Floyd placed the letter right in front of the clock face, to make sure he wouldn't forget to read it. When they finished with the watering he would turn up the lamp and wait for the boy to climb to his bunk. From up there the old man looked different, especially without his hat. He had most of his hair, but it lay flat on his skull and had the same color. At the back of his head the red lining of his cap had stained it orange. With his glasses on the boy thought his appearance very dignified.

"That Aunt of yours thinks I'm lost to the Devil!" he would say, as if he was pleased to hear it. His Aunt really thought no such thing; was that what she meant by scalawag? The boy gathered it was a person with an ornery streak, who pretty much did as he pleased.

"You attending, boy?" he would say. The boy had learned to be attending.

My dearest boy, your Auntie's batteries are not so low she can't say her own prayers and write her own letters, which certain people who shall go nameless find it increasingly difficult to do. My girl has left me alone [she called her neighbor, Mrs. Gertheimer, her "girl"] and I'm lonesome for my loved ones. No, I do not send Xmas cards. If God had wanted the world to celebrate Christ's birth date he would have said so, and we'd know what day it is [Aunt Viola believed there was some doubt in this matter] and it would not be the horrible event that your darling Uncle assures me it is. And you must not send me

*chocolates. This old tabernacle won't take it anymore—
the Lord knows how I'm tempted—but make it dates if
you must send me something.*

*Your Auntie loves small animals better than big ones,
and she hopes the Lord will forgive her. A puppy came
into the yard—I was lying in the hammock—and when
I spoke to him he came cautiously forward, making funny
little puppy overtures and whimperings, to sort of feel
out my attitude about puppies—and when he realized
I was friendly [Floyd Warner said, "She means it was
friendly, to agree with attitude"], you never in your life
saw such a happy creature! He pranced and made such
happy little yelps I guessed he must be hungry ["She
always thinks any animal is hungry!" the Uncle said] and
gave him some food. He just wanted to gulp it up, pan
and all. It takes so little to make God's creatures happy
["That excludes you and me, boy! and don't you forget
it!"], one just knows the power that Satan has in the souls
of men. I'm enclosing a little booklet for you, dear boy,
and I want you to read it with your eyes and heart open.
The Lord will take care of you, wherever you are, if
you'll just let him. The trouble is our stubborn wills get
in the way so often, and the stubbornest will I ever set my
eyes on is our old scalawag! If he would just not be so
willful he could look forward to a life eternal ["God help
me!" cried Uncle Floyd] but I have not lost faith that he
will stop being so stubborn and let himself grow up.*

*You've a cousin in Viet Nam—did you know that?
Orien Moody, Ethel's boy. It wouldn't hurt for you to
pray for him, as I do. He writes as if there was nothing
so commonplace as a war. I love you dearly, boy, and
know that your mother has her eyes on you right at this
moment.*

"Just that's enough," said the old man with a sigh, "to give a person the creeps." He returned the letter to the envelope, then turned a few pages of the little booklet, "The Man You Must Know." He tossed it up to where the boy was lying. "You better read it, while you've still got the brains you were born with."

It was not lost on the boy that this was in the nature of his first compliment.

Three

IT IS SEVEN LONG BLOCKS, or about a twenty-minute walk, from the Live Oak Trailer Camp to the main post office. On a hot day it seems more like a mile, and on a cold day an offshore breeze is blowing, and there is usually some fog. Nevertheless, hot or cold, the old man and the boy take this walk once a week to post the letter to Aunt Viola. ("I can't tell you what it means to me, dearest boy, to find your letter in the box Monday morning.") Whether she can tell him or not, that's where the letter is going to be, or should be, if the U.S. Postal Service was not in the hands of dropouts, copouts, hippies, and politicians. Considering that it is, it's amazing it works as well as it does. The mail service is the one general topic Floyd Warner will discuss with anybody, which includes such extremes as Mr. Yawkey, in the service, and a potential employee, Kermit Oelsligle. The pay was bad, but in uncertain times the government managed to stay in business. Men walked farther daily, and received nothing for it, playing golf. Uncle Floyd's scorn was shared equally with the mysteries and abuses of the mail service, and the new Leisure World of fun and games. Rubio has a park with a shuffleboard alley, and a strip of green lawn where the oldsters play "bowls," and though the Uncle doesn't play himself he sometimes pauses to watch the others. His head wags. He looks all around for someone who finds it as funny as he does. If he's so smart, and he is, why doesn't he see that *he's* the one that's funny? The boy stays clear of him at such times, not wanting to be mistaken for his next of kin. What is so funny about old men playing bowls? "God-a-mighty, boy," Uncle Floyd says. "If you don't know that how can I explain it?" In any case, he doesn't. There is no better exercise than a good walk, although there may be better walks than the one they take. The palms are so high they cast no shade, and if the old man isn't careful he will step in some dog crap. He does not mince his words about dogs. The town has no law about unleashed dogs, there having been so few of them in the past, but the present population numbers in the thousands. They are free to wander, obstruct traffic, block open doorways, copulate in public, and endanger life and limb with their droppings, some of them pie size. What kind of dogs are they to turn their backs on the earth and prefer cement sidewalks? The food they eat out of cans makes the smell of it worse. Floyd Warner dislikes all of this so much he complains to the Sheriff, if he can find him (he might be in his car, listening to the ball game), but as a rule he has to settle for Mr. Yawkey in the post office. Yawkey is old enough to have known better times, and smarter dogs. He is not important enough, however, to have any influence in the matter, and Uncle Floyd believes he is fearful of speaking his mind, if he has one. He has a job. He has no jurisdiction over unleashed dogs. The important thing about Mr. Yawkey's job is that he is paid to stand at the open stamp window, where Floyd Warner, or anybody else, can engage him in a discussion that may or may not have to do with the mails.

It comes to more than that. Mr. Yawkey is the one man in Rubio, available on call at the stamp window, who is actually part of the mindless forces that are taking over the country. Neither insult nor discussion will draw him out. On the other hand, neither does he walk off and start sorting letters at the back of the room. He stands there, his pale face green in the shadow of his visor, the shirtsleeves turned back on his hairless arms. As many as eight or ten pens—ballpoints, felt points, etc.—fit into a plastic holder that protects his shirt pocket, although the only pen the boy has seen him use lies on the metal counter with several rubber stamps. Now and then he takes a puff of the cigarette he balances on the rim of the scales, right over one of the pouches, and there is no way to explain why the place hasn't burnt down.

Not to obstruct public service Floyd Warner will stand to the left of the window, near the mail slots, sharing the remarks he directs to Mr. Yawkey with whomever he is doing business. Not many seem to mind. Many agree with his comments on the state of the Union. It was at this window that Floyd Warner had his first confrontation with the postal service. Mr. Yawkey (looking very much the same, but not so thick around the middle) refused to insure the package wrapped in the manner he had received it. (Insufficient twine, he said, or something foolish like that.) Floyd Warner, naturally, had threatened to complain to the Postmaster General, whose picture hung on the wall. It was at this point that Mr. Yawkey said something crucial.

"Mr. Varner," he said (misreading the name Warner on the package), "all I do is work here." A simple fact, of course, but a mistake for him to have said so. He has had to live with it for sixteen years. "I know all you do is work here, Mr. Yawkey—" he has heard Floyd Warner say at least once a week, and all things considered his temperament is still good, even sunny. If Floyd Warner actually *misses* a Friday, Mr. Yawkey is the first one to know it. When the mailman on the route comes back to the P.O. he asks him, "How's the old man, o-kay?"

If the seven-block walk is not constitutional, why does the old man take it? There is a large red and blue mailbox on the corner where he stands, daily, directing crossing traffic. It is tilted slightly, leaning forward, as if waiting for the light to change. The mail is picked up daily, rain or shine, at five o'clock. This metal box has legs equipped with bolt holes, so that it can be bolted to the curb or sidewalk, but it actually occupies the corner with no more assurance than its own weight, which is not much. Boys have accidentally moved it, playing tag, and purposely transported it on Halloween to one of many corners without one, a federal offense. Into this "litter" can (it has been used for that, too, and on at least one occasion half filled with water to which goldfish were added) Floyd Warner is expected to drop the weekly letter to his sister Viola? It beggars belief, one of many expressions he owes to her. Nothing has been done to improve this situation (as if painting it red and blue would improve it!) in all the years Floyd Warner has lived here, which is why he will walk, come hell or high water, to the post office itself to mail a letter. It's an outing for the boy, who walks ahead eating a Dixie Cup fudge sundae.

Rubio's business district is a block from the beach, with an area of benches and trees that cars are not allowed to enter. This had all been done before the hippie invasion and there was no legal way to keep them out of it. They took naps on the benches. They gathered in a cluster under the trees. In order to get them out of the Mall, the merchants let them have the empty Penny Arcade building. It had neither a wall nor windows at the front, and the boy could look in and see real hippies seated at the tables, talking, smoking, and eating. Food cooked by hippies was spread out on a counter, under a menu painted on the wall, like a mural. A meat loaf sandwich could be bought for twenty-five cents. The boy understood that if he ate such food he would get hepatitis and turn yellow. He didn't want to turn yellow, or worse than yellow, bleached out to white like a fish's belly. Not that it mattered too much, since he seldom had the twenty-five cents. What he liked to do was just stand there and look. If he stood in the ninth grade section of the schoolyard some smart aleck would tell him to go back where he came from, but no hippie would ask him to do anything as foolish as that. While Uncle Floyd went to speak to Mr. Yawkey, which might occupy him for twenty or thirty minutes, the boy would stand at the front of the Open Grave as if he was waiting for somebody. He saw plenty. He could fill a book with what he saw. He didn't hear much because the rock music made it impossible to hear anything else. If someone said, "Hi, man," to him, and it was not a girl, he would say, "Hi, man," back to him. Clear at the back of the room was a lavatory he had gone into and found a girl there, combing her hair. "Hi," she had said to him in the mirror. "Hi," he had said, washed his hands, and left. They smoked *grass* back there, and the one coming out would give the joint to the one coming in. He could fill a book with what he saw if he could be sure his Aunt Viola wouldn't find it and read it. She read a good deal, there being little else for her to do in bed.

If the weather was bad the hippies sometimes hung sheets at the front of the store to keep the wind and rain out. They kept the boy out, too, and he would either go down to the Thrifty Drugstore and read the comic books on the magazine rack, or go back to the side hall in the P.O. building and look at the pictures of the men Most Wanted by the FBI. Hardly any of these men had beards or long hair. The boy was shy about looking at *Wanted* people (wouldn't he shy off if they were looking for *him?*) until he found that not one of these people, as hard as he looked, ever looked back at him. They faced him. But at no time did he catch a look. These men were always alias one thing or another, which he could easily understand from the pictures, the same person looking one way from the front, another from the side. He would not himself have believed it was the same person, and wondered if the photographer might have got them mixed. These pictures of Wanted men were across the hall from the Army and Navy recruitment office, where an Army man, with his coat off, usually sat doing crossword puzzles. The office had a pair of scales against one wall, and a chart with large and small letters for checking the boys' eyes. He could read it all, easy, even from where he stood in the hallway. The one thing uncertain was how much the Army would want him to weigh. On the scale in the drugstore he weighed ninety-seven, which was up nine pounds from what he weighed in March. In the Army if he grew out of his clothes he would be able to get more free.

All of the stamp windows, those with metal grilles and the big one with the scales, operated by Mr. Yawkey, were just inside the lobby doors on the front. The boy took special pains to get in and out of the doors without being seen by Mr. Yawkey. Why was that? Mr. Yawkey never failed to flick him a friendly, conspiratorial wink. The boy agreed, almost without reservation, that Mr. Yawkey had lost what little brains he had been born with, but in one way or another he could not explain he still had more than Uncle Floyd. He could wink. He could share with the boy a joke about the old man. It embarrassed the boy to share this sort of knowledge with a person as dumb as Mr. Yawkey, who naturally assumed he was smarter than Uncle Floyd. His Uncle would be there, just off to one side if Mr. Yawkey was doing business, or leaning in the window to make remarks about how to improve the mail service. Mr. Yawkey no longer took this personally. At one time he did, and would slam down his window when he saw Floyd Warner come through the door, but that had got him nowhere since the Uncle would stay right there till the window was opened. The Uncle's point had been that he refused to pay taxes for the delivery of mail well known to be junk, and Mr. Yawkey's point had been that the U.S. mail service could not make an exception for Floyd Warner. This meant that Floyd Warner turned back all mail addressed to OCCUPANT, which was nearly all of it, and the local mailman, Mr. Dexter, often carried away more mail than he delivered. If he wouldn't take it away, Uncle Floyd would dump it in the "litter" box on the corner, where it would have to be sorted out in the post office. That was how it had begun. Over the years, however, Uncle Floyd had got tired of writing *Return to Sender* on so many junk letters (if he didn't, he got them back two days later) and just let them collect in a cereal carton and threw it out when it was full, about once a month. His argument with Mr. Yawkey was more of a discussion growing out of different views of the Postal Service, one from the inside, which was pretty complicated, and the other from the outside, which was getting worse. One of Uncle Floyd's beefs was the female hippie who delivered early Special Deliveries in her nightshirt, a point that Mr. Yawkey considered well taken, and saw that it was stopped. What the boy waited to hear (out of sight but not earshot) was the slap of the old man's hand on the counter, which signals that he is preparing to leave.

"I don't want the Postmaster General, Mr. Yawkey, to think you've got nothing to do but entertain the public!"

The boy tried to sneak out while Mr. Yawkey turned to wink at one of the mail sorters, or stood tossing packages into the mail pouches at his back. That had once been a sore point with Uncle Floyd, but he no longer mentioned it.

On their way back to the camp Uncle Floyd might buy a pint of French vanilla, to eat on sliced peaches, since the long walk gave them both a bigger appetite. He also felt more like eating if he got a few real gripes off his chest.

Four

FLOYD WARNER KEPT a calendar on which he jotted
what sort of day it was, every day of the year. Windy,
overcast, drizzly, rain, clear and cool, clear and warm,
and all through October he put simply, *Dandy*. Prac-
tically every day was dandy, and that had been true
over the years. They might get a few gale winds up
from the south, and maybe patches of morning fog
along the coast, but day after day it was weather to
suit the creator. The boy thought that an odd way for
the old man to put it, with his feelings on the subject
what they were, but he spelled creator with a small *c*,
and meant no nonsense. Something had to have started
the whole shooting match, and that was what he called
the creator. It stirred in him reverence and awe, but

mostly awe. He could experience this by looking at the sky, and the veil-like scarf of the Milky Way, and he could also experience it closer at hand by lowering his eyes and gazing at the ground. Years ago he had done that, while herding sheep, having very little else to do. He had sat down on a rock, and let his eyes rest on the small hole of some earth creature. Not so big as a prairie dog hole, or a mouse hole, but somewhat larger than most ant holes. Heaped around it, as in most cases, were the sand and pebbles kicked up out of the hole. A tiny volcano: that was how it would look in a photograph. He was struck by the color of one of the pebbles, and took a closer look. Separated from the others, in the palm of his hand, it looked very much like the stub of a pencil, only not so large. One end of it was sharpened to a very fine point, and it had six smooth polished sides. The other end was just a crude stump of dirt and sand, as if left unfinished.

At that point along the valley of the Pecos River Floyd Warner was twenty miles from the road, and about a mile from the shack he lived in. No one had passed that way before, so far as he knew. In the distant past there had surely been Indians: had one of them fashioned it for an arrowhead, or some sort of tool? It was a very great puzzle to Floyd Warner, but not, to his mind, a mystery. Someone had made it as it was, and for a reason. One day he would know. In the next few weeks, his eyes searching for ground holes, he found more than a dozen of these strange objects. A few were perfectly finished off at both ends. Some were tiny as beads, others as thick as pencils. All colors, but he thought it one kind of stone. He soon had a small coin purse full of these gems, and when he brought his herd back from their grazing he showed them to an old-timer in Carlsbad. He had seen them many times. "Pecos Diamonds" were what they were called. They weren't really diamonds, of course, and not worth anything on the market, but they were found all along the Pecos and always had that particular shape. Who had made them? Aunt Viola and people like her were quick to say they were made by the Lord. They showed His hand. But they didn't show at all what His hand was about. The proper question was *what* made them?—and in time Uncle Floyd had his answer. He showed them to a mining engineer in Roswell and this man immediately described them as "crystals," said that *nobody* had made them, but in the nature of things they just made themselves. He used the word "snowflakes." Rain needed to turn colder for snow, but rocks needed great heat to become crystals. It was a matter of temperature, not the mysterious hand of God. Understandably, the Uncle had shown the boy a pouchful of these objects, and had been pleased to see the boy's eyes widen, his jaw hang slack. That was awe, much to be preferred to reverence. The boy was privately certain Indians had made them, but he was not so foolish as to say so. "Goddam it to hell, boy, didn't I just tell you *what* they were?" He thought they were great, whoever made them, and for keeping his mouth shut he had one of his own, not quite so fine as the others, but every bit as hard to explain. He had shown this example to the four or five people he thought bright enough to appreciate it, two of them girls. One of the girls, Eileen, wanted him to drill a hole in it, put a string through it, and let her wear it, if he wouldn't himself. She was certain anything made by Indians would bring you luck. The boy liked beads, even strung beads, but he surely knew better than to wear beads, or let *any*body drill a hole in his rock. He kept it in the watch pocket of his jeans, and it had already been twice through the laundry. One day he would have it polished, put it in a ring, and send it to Aunt Viola. He would say he had found it. It was all right with him if she believed it was made by the hands of the Lord.

The boy's best friend was Manuel Gonzales, whose father was janitor of the grade school. Manuel came early to school, then stayed late in order to ride his mini-bike in the empty playground. He could ride in a circle with the handlebars spinning, or jerk the front wheel up and ride around on the rear wheel, like an acrobat. The only person he allowed to ride his bike was the boy. All he did was ride around the playground while Manuel sat on the exercise bars and watched him. "You ride good," he said to Kermit, who had shared with him a close look at the "diamond." His only observation had been that it looked like a "doll's tit," but had no taste. Manuel dipped popsicle sticks in ketchup and sucked on them as he rode around on his bike. He envied Kermit living in a trailer and showed no interest at all in his being an orphan, or why his Uncle Floyd, his next of kin, happened to be so old. Mrs. Todd, his teacher, considered Kermit a nice clean boy, with good manners, but less carefree than most boys of his age. "Are you happy?" she asked him, hoping he would say yes, but his eyes filled with tears and he couldn't speak. Not that he was *un*happy, but he did seem to miss the rides in the pickup, with his father, the dog Schroeder sitting between them so that he looked like a hippie girl from the rear. Every evening they rode out to look at the steers, white-faced and clean in the green feed lots, the air sweet with the smell of the sprinklers and bundled hay. It was understood between them that the father talked to his son through Schroeder, eliminating the sort of confrontation they both had with the mother. Not wanting Schroeder's fleas, she had stopped riding with them in the cab.

He was not unhappy—one of the trailer ladies paid

him one dollar a week to walk her Doberman pinscher where he wouldn't see other dogs or frighten people. The dog had had an operation on his ears, and looked to other dogs like a giant rabbit. The boy spent this money on cream soda and potato chips. On Saturday nights the hippies had a rock concert at Adelphi Hall, four blocks west on Shoreline, which the boy could listen to like the carnival music he had heard in Palmdale, the lights on the Ferris wheel visible from where he lay in bed. He understood from what Mrs. Leidy said, and others, that his Uncle Floyd had been quite a "cutup" when they held the square dances in Santa Cruz, until his knee got tricky, and he had to give it up. What people did now he did not consider dancing, or anything else. The boy was privately of two minds about hippies, not wanting, at any cost, to be mistaken for a girl, but very much attracted to beads, bare feet, and far-out hats. He liked their talk. He looked forward to hearing someone call him *man*.

The boy was back from school, in the kitchen of the trailer, concealed behind the refrigerator door he had opened, when he saw the mailman approach and slip a letter under the screen. His mouth full of Fig Newtons, he made no sound. The mailman went away without knocking, and he saw the letter was a telegram, the name Floyd Warner behind the glassine window of the envelope. He wondered what had happened. He understood that telegrams were always bad news. He put it on the table, where his Uncle would see it, then decided he should go and tell him about it. At this hour of the day, he was the crossing guard at the playground exit. The boy did not mosey toward him, playing with his yo-yo, but walked right down and stood at the corner. His Uncle was surprised to see him, but let him wait. Having a message to deliver distracted the boy from what the Uncle was doing, and how silly he looked. He was also a person of some importance to receive a telegram. When he didn't cross over, but just stood there, the old man said, "Well, boy, what is it?"

"You got a telegram."

"I got what?"

"You got a telegram. The mailman brought it."

"Why didn't you bring it?"

The boy had no idea. It simply hadn't crossed his mind to bring it. "Should I go get it?"

No, he didn't want it. He had only a few more minutes to go, and then they could both go back and read it. "A telegram?" he repeated. "Who sent it?"

How would the boy know that? He began to feel the urgency, however, and the five-minute wait seemed a long time. "Skeedaddle!" said the old man to the last child, and gave her a thump in the rear with his Stop sign. Without going to the storage box to change his jacket, he led the boy back to the trailer, the Stop sign still in his hand when he stepped inside. He held the envelope to the light at the window, turning it one way then another, straining to read it.

"Why don't you *open* it?" asked the boy.

"I think I know," said the old man. Did he think that was an answer? "It's your Aunt," he said. "Something to do with your Aunt."

The boy had guessed it was from Aunt Viola. Who else? His Uncle put the telegram on the table, then sat down. Between his legs he held the Stop sign, gripping the metal rim with both hands.

"Aren't you going to read it?"

"You read it," the old man replied.

That was how the boy was the first to really know that his Aunt Viola had passed away in her sleep. Arrangements were pending, and they wanted instructions wired. The boy wondered what sort of instructions, and where they would have to go to wire them, but her brother, Floyd Warner, said nothing whatsoever, his face concealed by the hard hat. The boy felt embarrassed to see his Uncle's stubborn will bend like a branch under Aunt Viola's faith, who was already up where she said she would be, watching them both.

Later that evening the boy and his Uncle walked the seven blocks to the Western Union office, where the Uncle wired that Viola Warner should be buried in the plot with the rest of the family, if there was room. If there was not room, as near to it as she could get. This still left twenty-three words in a night letter so he said he would be coming to settle her affairs as soon as he could make the proper arrangements. At nine-thirty, the usual time, they were both in bed. The boy tried not to think of Aunt Viola, up in heaven, because he knew that his Uncle would not be there. He would be in the other place, wherever that was, wearing his yellow hard hat, his orange jacket, and holding up his Stop sign to people like the boy who might want to get in.

Mrs. Leidy advised him that he could fly there and back in less than twelve hours. She had flown to Oklahoma, attended a funeral, and visited friends in Fort Mills, Arkansas, then returned to Rubio in less than three days.

Or:

Traveling by bus, he could leave Monday morning, be there on Thursday, and then back by Monday, seeing much of America in the comfort of an air-conditioned coach.

Or:

The City of San Francisco left Oakland at ten in the morning, then went through the Feather River Canyon and across Nevada, Utah, through the heart of the Rockies along the Colorado River to arrive in

Lincoln just before midnight, if it was on time. In the morning a bus would then take him back to Chapman in about two hours.

At least it was one thing or the other, Mrs. Leidy said, since no man of his age should try to drive it. Drive it? Uncle Floyd might have forgotten that he could drive it if Mrs. Leidy hadn't brought it up, it had been so long since the Maxwell had been off the blocks.

Floyd Warner liked to sleep on major decisions, but he lay awake most of the night on this one. The boy could hear him scratching himself, and smacking his lips. In the morning his mind was made up, however, and he woke the boy to tell him. "Get up, boy," he said, giving him a shake. "We got to get packed."

It had taken him all night to sort things out and understand what had happened back in Chapman. Aunt Viola could be buried, in one plot or another, and rise as she knew she would to heaven, but there remained the house in which she had lived all but a few years of her life. As the family died off they had left things with her, and now there was no one left but Floyd Warner. Himself and the boy. Soon there would be only the boy. If Kermit Oelsligle had the brains he was born with on his mother's side of the family, he would see that something had to be done, and know what it was. But he didn't seem to.

"Goddam it to hell!" the old man shouted. "Don't you know who you are?"

"I'm Aunt Viola's boy," he replied.

That surprised Floyd Warner. The boy stared at him through a blur of tears. If he blinked they would run down his face, so he stared without blinking.

"Blow your nose!" the old man said, handing him the dish towel. "We've got a lot to do."

What they had to do first was take the tarpaulin off the car and get the battery charged. The Maxwell coupe still had its original paint, a dark-green color, but it had crackled to look like imitation leather. On the right side running board were three cans, in a rack, painted red, white, and blue, for gas, water, and oil. Experience had taught the Uncle to put water in them all. The smartest thing he had ever done was install an electric starter when he had the motor overhauled in the forties, since he was now too old, and the boy was still too young, to crank it. Without the trailer in tow, the car had last made a run up the California coast to Seal Beach, near Portland, where Floyd Warner had once been tempted by a bit of land speculation. He had decided against it when an earthquake gave the whole area a shake. The Maxwell even had a heater in the cab, but it was not very effective until the water was hot. If the water got hot they would have bigger problems than cold feet. While the battery was charging, the boy pumped up the tires. The two on the rear of the coupe were new when Uncle Floyd had driven to Seal Beach, but the other four, counting two on the trailer, were smooth as bicycle tires. Two of them they could use as spares, but what they needed were four new tires for such a long trip. The boy reasoned that if they were going to buy tires, why didn't they let the tire people put in the air—which was just the kind of reasoning his Uncle expected from a boy who had never done a day's work in his life. These tires were on rims, and it was something of a problem to get the tire off the rim, even with tire irons, and nobody in the tire business today would go around the corner to replace a tire, or do that kind of work. The boy saw that if the rims were slipped off the wheels he could *roll* the rim and tire the mile to the tire shop, but since he *did* have the brains he was born with he did not make this suggestion. He pumped ten pounds of air into each of the tires, and let it go at that. Packing the trailer was no problem—after all, it was already packed—but getting it and the car down off the blocks proved to be a headache. In the entire trailer camp there were only two jacks of the sort you could stick under an axle. The new style jack wouldn't fit on the Maxwell, or raised the cab in the air and left the wheels on the blocks. They were all set to go but they couldn't get the wheels down on the ground.

The Uncle would fool around beneath it with the jack, thumping his head, then he would get up and stand off to one side, where he could see the whole rig, and soberly curse it. Some of the men had heard such language, but the ladies in the camp said they had never heard it. He didn't raise his voice much: he just folded his arms and went on and on. The problem was solved by five of the men using one of the railroad ties as a lever, lifting the Maxwell just enough to slide out the blocks. The trailer could just be pulled off, once they got the Maxwell motor started. Mr. Gonzales, the janitor, who worked part time at a gas station in the summer, went home for his supper, then came back and stayed until after dark, when he got it started. He advised putting in five gallons of gas and letting it run. The Maxwell motor had a good even sound when it idled, but it wouldn't idle without backfiring. First it would cough two or three times, then go off like a bomb. Someone in the camp called the Highway Patrol, who pointed out that the car had a four-year-old license, and lucky for him it was not out on the road. Lucky for him also, Floyd Warner proved to have his car ownership papers in his green metal file with Aunt Viola's letters, but unlucky for him his driver's license was four years out of date. Taking care of all of that took three days, since he flunked his first two driver's tests, but it allowed time for Mr. Gonzales to get the motor in tune and reduce the backfire. It also gave the boy time to study the map and figure out that it was 1,948 miles from where they were to where they were going, following the route the man in the gas station laid out. At a cruising speed of thirty miles an hour they would hope to do two hundred miles a day, most of it early in the morning, before the desert sun got hot. Long trips by car were not new to Uncle Floyd, who had once been all the way to Guadalajara, but he had given up traveling when the freeways made it all one big racetrack. Did he think it had changed? No, he did not, but this was a trip that couldn't be helped. He was through with traveling. He and the boy were going home. Thanks to the awful freeways, once they were north of San Francisco they could go all the way without big city traffic, free to pull off the road and eat and sleep where they chose. They would leave at dawn, going north along the coast, and before the morning traffic was jamming up the city they would be crossing the bridge, over the Golden Gate, considered by the Uncle to be one of the seven wonders of the world. Those situated in far-off, superstitious places he considered out of date.

Book Two

One

EVEN THE BEST-LAID PLANS may fail to take into account the early-morning traffic in San Francisco, where Uncle Floyd, confused by two bridges, ended up taking the wrong one to Oakland, three miles long with no place he could turn off. A Highway Patrol car with the blinker revolving followed them across.

"Pop," he said, "you're under the limit."

Uncle Floyd was certain he had heard it wrong. They had been going twenty-five, maybe less, in a thirty-five-mile-limit zone.

"You got to go *over* it, Pop," said the cop.

"Boy," said Uncle Floyd, "it won't *go* over thirty-five!"

He proved to be a nice, friendly cop, however, and

gave them directions instead of a ticket. What they should do was get off the freeway until the traffic let up. The cop went ahead of them to a freeway exit where they could drive under thirty and not get arrested. To help pass the time until the traffic let up, they had their second breakfast in a Richmond diner, where they could also park on one meter at the curb. The cook in the diner, who lived in Vallejo, explained how to drive under thirty on the freeway. They should stay over to the right as if they were preparing to get off. If a cop stopped them for slowing up the traffic, they would simply tell him they were pulling off. If they had to pull off, they would get back on and do the same thing. Once they got to Sacramento the road got wider and there were lanes for slow traffic on the grades. To be on the safe side, in case they had to pull off where there was no place to park, and nothing to eat, they let the cook make them up a bag of sandwiches. Highway travel had changed since Uncle Floyd had come west in 1941.

They were back in the car, looking for the freeway entrance, when the boy noticed the paper under the windshield wiper. A ticket? He decided to ignore it. If they were leaving the state the cops would never find them. But when they pulled into a station to ask directions the attendant found it and had a look at it.

"Hey, look at this!" he said. "You got a cash offer."

"I got what?" said Uncle Floyd, but he couldn't read it, and passed it on to the boy. Someone had written

For CASH OFFER call
Wilner 386-9886

on the back of a canned tuna fish wrapper.

"Cash for what?" Uncle Floyd asked.

"Your car, Pop. People collect old cars."

Uncle Floyd didn't believe such nonsense for a moment.

"They might give you even more than you paid for it," said the attendant, "in case it's paid for." He gave the boy a wink.

"God-a-mighty, boy," he said, "now why would I sell it? I'd only have to go and buy me another."

"I've one I'll sell you for three seventy-five," said the attendant. "All it needs is tires."

"Young man," said Uncle Floyd, "you may take me for a fool, but I'm not see-nile!"

"If I were you I'd keep the offer," he replied, "just in case."

"If you were me, boy," Uncle Floyd said, "you wouldn't." But since they were there he let him put in five gallons of gas.

The traffic on the freeway was still pretty bad, but they fell in behind a truck pulling a wide house trailer, with flags out on the side. The truck's speed averaged about twenty-five, and cut down on the wind. They tagged right along behind him through Sacramento, where a new, wider freeway led into the mountains, and the old man called the boy's attention to the color of the leaves. Born and raised in California, as he had been, he had little or no idea of the change of the seasons, the whiteness of the winter, or what it was like to look forward to spring. It led him to ask the boy what, if anything, he looked forward to. Just as he feared, the boy didn't know. He looked forward, that's all. If it was evening, he looked forward to morning. If it was Monday, he looked forward to Saturday, and that sort of thing. He just looked forward. Where else was there to look?

Uncle Floyd said he was thankful to hear what he said, since it surely confirmed what he feared the worst. California was a place to grow old and die in, but not grow up. He, Floyd Warner, was of the opinion, having lived for some years in both places, that no man on whom the snow did not fall was worth a hill of beans. While there was still time the boy had damn well better get himself under it. The boy had heard this before, but not so well put, and in this context it left a stronger impression. If people were divided between those on whom it snowed, and those on whom it didn't, it would prove to be a help in sorting them out. Snow had fallen on his mother (no way to tell about his father), on his Aunt Viola, on his Uncle Floyd, and once it had all but buried his grandfather, who had been found with a pack of ice in his hair. It may have frozen his wits, but it didn't kill him, and he had gone on to preach his religious nonsense, the snow, unfortunately, not being a cure for some human ills. The boy would do well to keep all of this in mind when the time came for him to choose a wife between some female with her brains sunbaked, her hair the color of baled hay, or some woman with skin like snow, and the sun in her heart. The boy slept on it, his head lolling from side to side, as the cab tilted, but his eyes were open when they rounded a curve and there, up ahead of them, were two people. Snow might have once fallen on the young man with the beard, but the girl had hair like a bale of hay, and almost as long. The young man carried a pack on his back, and had thin, hairy legs.

"They hitchhikers?" His Uncle did not reply, his gaze far up the road as if he didn't see them. The girl wore stockings of a purple color and a skirt so short she didn't seem to have one. Her long hair hung below it. About her shoulders she wore a green shawl. The boy had never seen a girl with a bigger, friendlier smile.

The old man said, "No hitchhikers. About half of them just as soon shoot you."

As the car came up and went by them the boy

thought the young man looked familiar. His expression was sad. His black beard came to a point on his chin. The girl put up her arm and waved to the boy; he waved back.

"Besides," Uncle Floyd said, "we've got no room. It's against the law to ride in a trailer." In the side mirror the boy saw the young man put a thumb to his nose and wiggle his fingers at them, then the curve of the road cut the two of them from view.

Just before dark Uncle Floyd discovered that the lights didn't work. He cursed elegantly for about five minutes and walked around the car giving the lights a hard thump. But none of that helped. Uncle Floyd was knowledgeable about the magneto, the distributor, and the carburetor, but anything to do with electric wiring he preferred to leave to other people. But not Mr. Gonzales. He had always found that people full of good will seldom proved to know their ass from a hole in the ground. In fixing one thing they managed to ruin something else. Fortunately, the lamp in the trailer used gas, and the boy walked back down the road and held it. A young man in a Chevy pickup stopped by to help them, but he was not familiar with a car so old.

"You should be lucky it runs," he said. "What do you want, everything?" He meant that as a joke, of course, but his Uncle didn't laugh. What he *could* do for them was fall in behind and flash his high beams far up the freeway. That way Uncle Floyd could see where he was going, and they drove along on the tail of their shadow. About ten miles ahead they reached a camp for trailers, where they could stop for the night.

The camp had no lights of its own, but it was all lit up by Mr. Cowles' mobile home. He and Mrs. Cowles were traveling west to visit Disneyland and see their grandchildren. Mrs. Cowles had retired the moment they arrived because winding mountain roads always left her queasy. She sat in their living room watching the news on the TV. Mr. Cowles was not much help with their lights either, but he was very much impressed with Uncle Floyd's Maxwell. Not himself, but his father had owned a Dodge touring that he couldn't seem to wear out and became very fond of, driving it around during all those years when new cars were scarce. Mr. Cowles would never forget the characteristic ping the old Dodge motor made. He would say to his wife, "Here he comes, Laura," two or three minutes before he pulled in the yard. In 1949 he turned it in on a Plymouth, which he drove till his death. Even his father, however, would never have dreamed of driving that car across the mountains, and pulling a trailer with it. What he proposed to do was take some Polaroid snapshots of Uncle Floyd, and the

Maxwell, in the morning, which he would send back to have printed in the *Motor Trails News*, in Racine, Wisconsin. They ran a special section on antique cars every month. He personally believed this was the first antique he had ever actually seen pulling a trailer, but there might be others in out-of-the-way places, and parts of the South. In the morning, when the light was better, he would take some shots. He and Mrs. Cowles had started their trip with their dog, but somewhere in Wyoming he had taken off and left them, all of which proved, in Mrs. Cowles' opinion, that he had more sense than they did. She didn't care much for campers. If she ever took a trip like this again, she said, it would be in a box.

During the night Uncle Floyd decided he didn't want pictures of either himself or the Maxwell, so they were up before it was light and left the camp without eating breakfast. A few miles down the road they pulled off the freeway rather than go through the tunnel up ahead without lights. A rancher going west, with two crates of leghorn pullets, stopped to see if they were having trouble. His own car was a '37 Ford V-8 so he knew what to expect when he lifted the hood. "You've blown a fuse," he said, fiddling around, and used the one they had blown, wrapped in a piece of tinfoil from his cigarette package, to make one that would work. The way the Maxwell worked, they had really good lights when they raced the motor, and not so good when they didn't. But there was always light enough so the people coming toward them could see them.

Although the road was new, and the boy had the impression they were cruising along on the level, the radiator boiled every ten or twelve miles and made the windshield a solid rust color. It might take the boy a quarter of an hour to get a bucket of water from the shallow river. Ten miles farther it would all go up in steam and spray. One thing it did was clean out all the rust, so the spray on the windshield also helped to clean it. But they took almost all day getting over the pass. On the far side of the mountains they could coast, and almost get back the gas they had wasted, but the old man was so tired he couldn't stay awake. He thought it best to stop and take a little nap, which proved to be until morning, and the sun woke him up. He swore to the boy he had never in his life slept so long as that. They both woke up hungry, and the boy was collecting firewood when he heard someone yelling at him from the freeway. The girl with the long hair, all of it wildly blowing, sat at the rear of a truck with her legs dangling, giving him her big, friendly smile and waving her arm. The boy waved back. The young man was seated out of the wind with his knees drawn up, his head resting on his arms.

"Who was that, boy?"

"That was them," he replied, but the old man didn't ask him for an explanation. The truck had been used for hauling hay or straw because bits of chaff blew in the windstream behind it, one of the girl's brown legs swinging in front of the taillight so it seemed to blink.

Two

In the morning the boy was up to see the sunrise behind what he thought must be the Rocky Mountains, they looked so far away. The old man had planned for them to leave about daylight, but he hadn't slept well with the soreness in his legs, and the noise in his ears. He didn't notice this crackling, like bacon frying, till he put his head on the pillow. Then it went on all night. The boy had heard his own ears go pop, but he would rather they did that than do nothing at all. It was part of traveling, like the nose-bleed he had in the men's room. He was doing nothing more than just looking at himself, when his nose began to bleed. He was ashamed to face his Uncle with his nose bleeding, so he sat in one of the booths, his head tipped way back, swallowing all the blood he would otherwise be losing, till it finally stopped. But something like that was what you had to expect when you were traveling around.

Another thing about traveling: if you would like to save money, what you do is always order some sort of breakfast. His Uncle Floyd might eat eggs three times a day, boiled in the morning, hard boiled for lunch, and fried hard in the evening, but since *he* didn't like eggs he ate hotcakes in the morning, cold cereal for lunch, and maybe hotcakes for supper with a piece of ham. They had planned to eat in the trailer, which they could do on about half the money, but after riding all day they both liked to get out and walk around the town, then eat in a diner. If he couldn't walk somewhere to eat, his Uncle Floyd would rather not eat at all. Only walking took the kink out of his legs that seemed to be there every time he stood up, and made him so stiff and sore in the morning he could hardly move. The foot he used on the gas pedal would go to sleep for so long he couldn't feel the pedal. If he took off his boots his feet would swell so he could hardly get them on in the morning. Was he feeling his years? He asked himself that when he thought the boy was out of earshot. It was also better to stop every hour or so than drive for three or four hours, then take a nap for six. Once he really fell asleep right after lunch he couldn't seem to wake up. Some of that might be caused by the elevation, as Mr. Cowles had mentioned back in the mountains, but most of it, in Uncle Floyd's opinion, came from sitting too much "at the goddam wheel." Just gripping the wheel made his fingers so swollen he could hardly butter his toast in the morning, or pick up a spoon. Added to that, the noise and rattle of the cab went on all night, as if trapped in his ears. It was too goddam bad, the old man said, that the boy wasn't just a year or two older, which was not exactly old enough to drive but surely big enough to sit at the wheel out here in the open where he hardly had to do anything else. The boy replied that he *had* sat at the wheel, and even more than that he had once shifted the gears in his father's pickup. It had been his father's custom to let him sit at the wheel and move the car if time ran out on the parking meter. He was older and bigger now than he was then by more than a year. The old man said if he could just sit, and not drive, he wouldn't have the kink problems in his legs, and it would not be necessary for them to lose five hours while he took a nap. At the rate they were going, ninety miles a day, it might even be snowing before they reached Nebraska, where a blizzard in November was every bit as common as roses in May. So what happened was, about three miles out of Lovelock, the old man stopped the car and slid over in the seat, while the boy got out and walked around to climb in behind the wheel. His legs were almost as long. His brown hands looked good on the wheel. He put in the clutch, he pulled back the shift, and he let it out so slow they both thought it was slipping, then it caught, and without even a lurch they were off.

"Can you stop it, boy?"

Yes, he could stop it. Unfortunately, he also killed the motor. But that was because he was inexperienced, and the old man watching him made him nervous. There was nothing to it. He felt he would like to drive both day and night. "If the town's big enough to have lights, we stop, and I take over. You understand that, boy?"

The next town with lights had so many the boy could see them from miles away. An airplane beacon swept the cooling sky. The old man had been dozing, his head on a pillow, and when the car stopped moving the quiet woke him up. It took him a moment to remember where they were. "That Lordsburg?" he said, sitting up.

The boy had never heard of Lordsburg. The town ahead, according to the map, should be a place called Winnemucca. Winnuh—who? It was right there on the map. In Winnemucca there were gas stations with showers, and they both took one and felt a lot better.

The trailer camp provided ice water, and the boy had never before seen a slot machine. They walked through the door into a darkened room like a movie lobby, full of these machines, cranked by men and women. They had entered the building under a sign that said BREAKFAST AT ALL HOURS, but the boy was a minor, and minors were not allowed. Floyd Warner took exception to that, and said he and the boy would eat where they pleased to, which proved to be a smaller place farther down the street. The sky was lit up all night long by the blinking signs. That and the ice machine made it hard to sleep and they were not up at daylight as they had planned. The old man refused to wear dark glasses, and ruin a pair of eyes that had never caused him trouble, but the boy, now that he was driving, felt it important for him to see clearly. At eight in the morning he had the sun hot in his face. According to their new plan the old man would drive to the edge of town, out beyond the traffic, where he would stop and the boy would take over. He was ready. He wore the new glasses that made the brown desert almost look green. Thanks to them, surely, he was able to see the hitchhiker far down the road. She was no longer wearing the purple stockings, and appeared to have on nothing but her long hair. The boy thought she was out there in the desert, all alone, and he would surely have stopped if he had been driving, but when they were closer he saw the young man lying on his back in the ditch grass, his head resting on his pack. In order to get a good suntan he had taken off his shirt.

"That's them!" he cried, and he would have stopped, or at least slowed down, or something. For maybe four or five seconds, it might have been longer, the old man let his foot ease up on the pedal—then he saw who they were and pushed it flat to the floor. The girl waved both her arms and threw the boy a kiss when they went by. It didn't seem to bother her at all that they didn't stop. They were going up an incline, with the road so straight he could see them in the rear-view mirror for miles, the sun gleaming on her yellow hair. How did the pair of them always end up ahead, although the old man and the boy always passed them? Where were they going? Was it some sort of game? Floyd Warner didn't say one word or another, or even let on to the boy that he had seen them, but he drove the car for another hour just to make sure he had put them behind him. With the wind at their backs, they cruised along at almost forty miles an hour.

His Uncle took the wheel again, out of Elko, then the boy drove for more than four hours, once coming within an inch of falling asleep with the right wheel off in the gravel. It scared him awake, so that

after that he was all right. They had to have a confer-
ence in the city of Wells as to how they planned to
cross the Great Salt Lake desert, and on the advice of
the gas station attendant they bought a water bag and
let it ride on the fender. By sundown they had come
almost three hundred miles. Floyd Warner had hardly
driven any of it, but just riding all day had worn him
out. He wasn't hungry either, and went to bed while
the boy drank pop and ate two hamburgers. The clerk
in the store looked like Carlos Gonzales but the boy
guessed him to be an Indian. He read comic books and
made change from money in an ashtray. They were in
Utah, but the difference was not too noticeable. The
boy was able to see, from a rise he walked to, almost
all the way back to Nevada, where the girl with the
big warm smile was probably smiling at somebody.
She continued to do that even when people didn't stop.
This impressed him as unusual behavior that required
some sort of explanation, but he understood he was
not going to get it from the old man. He would like
to meet this girl in a filling station and ask where it
was they were going. That was not uncommon. They
had already been asked four or five times. If she continued to smile he would then ask her how they always
happened to be up ahead, right after the boy and his
Uncle had passed them. This would all be easier if he

was sitting at the wheel when they came into the station for a drink or something, and he could say to her, "Be seeing you!" knowing that he would.

They were still in Nevada when he saw, far up ahead, this roiling, mud-colored river obstructing the road. It proved to be sheep, thousands of them, and when he stopped the car they flowed around behind it and they could move neither forward nor backward. Mixed in with the flock were hundreds of invisible bleating lambs. Such a moiling sea of creatures gave the boy a fright, but Uncle Floyd got out of the car and waded in among them, clutching the wool on their backs. He could hear him shouting elegant curses, as if he knew some of them personally. The movement of the flock carried him along with them, as if he rode on their backs. If sheep were the dumbest things alive, as the boy had been told, why did the old man seem so fond of them? It was no accident, he said, that the Lord Jesus spoke of his followers as sheep. The huge flock was kept in order by several dogs that ran along beside the pack, as if stalking, their heads and tails kept low. The sheepherder himself, with a blanket roll on his back, was so far away the boy could hardly see him. In his excitement, clutching the sheep for support, the old man was carried off with them. Did he know what he was doing? Off maybe one hundred yards he wheeled around and cupped his hands to his face, as if shouting something. The boy heard nothing but the bleating lambs. The old man did not move— a single buffeted figure, a snag in the river that flowed wide and fast—but tried to hold his footing against the current. The boy leaned out the window, as from a bridge railing, shouting, "Uncle Floyd!" as if that would help. The old man held his place by reaching forward to clutch at the wool streaming toward him. The boy continued to holler. The lambs continued to bleat. In spite of his age the boy had never questioned that his Uncle Floyd could stand up to anything— even God, if necessary. Mr. Yawkey, Mrs. Leidy, the U.S. Postal Service, or a bus full of heathens could not budge him. Aunt Viola called this strength his stubborn will. Had it proved equal to everything but a flock of dumb sheep? The boy's fury was in part his dim awareness that he, too, was helpless. Against a force as mindless as this he could only rage. And then it was gone: he watched the tail end of the flock recede, leaving the old man high and dry in the desert, his back humped from the posture he had held while standing his ground. When the boy ran toward him, he waved him off. He needed no help from a pre-teen boy to get himself out of what he had got into. That was his point. He took his own good time coming back to the car, stooping here and there to pick up a few pebbles, but it was not lost on the boy that his hands were still trembling when he got to the car, his shirt tail stuck to his back. Some miles down the road the boy caught him sniffing the fingers of both hands, oily and smelly with the sheep wool. Did he like it? He made no complaint. The sheep stench had also rubbed off on his pants, so it was like having one in the cab with them. As strong as the smell the boy had the impression that his Uncle would have liked someone older to talk to, it not being every day that he was carried away by a flock of sheep. When they stopped for the night the hard-boiled egg his Uncle first peeled, then handed to him, had the taste of all that wool he had clutched. "You wear it off, boy," he said, catching his eye, "you don't wash it off."

Three

THEY TOOK OFF before sunrise, without breakfast; was
that why, in a long, long day, he didn't see them? Not
even once. He did manage to see the Great Salt Lake,
and sent a small bag of it to Manuel Gonzales, care of
his father, the janitor at the school. In the afternoon
heat, there being no shade, they both took naps lying
under the trailer. What it led him to discover was that
one tire had a wobbly spot that had worn through the
rubber. A new tire, but the wobble had worn it out.
The tire man at the station explained that the wobble
was not due to the wheel, but to the wag of the trailer,
and that it might not be an easy thing to correct. At
fifteen miles an hour it might not wag, but they would
be a long time getting where they were going. The

other thing they could do would be to buy a new tire every thousand miles.

While they were waiting for the tire to come out from Salt Lake City the boy sat in the station observing the travelers. Most of them took him for one of the natives, which he thought was fine. He was seated on the fender, beside the water cans, when Mr. Simpson, of Long Beach, spoke to him. He drove a Chrysler sedan with windows so dark it was difficult for the boy to see Mrs. Simpson, if that was who she was. She kept the windows up because the air-conditioner was on. Mr. Simpson had stopped to have his oil changed, which he liked to do regular as clockwork.

"What's that you got there, son?" he said to the boy, meaning the car.

"It's an antique," he replied, showing he was not born yesterday.

"I can see that for myself," Mr. Simpson said. "You think it ought to be pulling that trailer?"

"It's all right except for the wobble," the boy advised him.

Uncle Floyd had been resting inside the trailer, but hearing them talk he put his head out. "I'm Arthur Simpson, of Long Beach," Mr. Simpson said, "and I've been having a chat with your boy."

"He never talks with me," the old man replied. "What did he say?"

"He was saying you had a little trailer wobble. You know, that's hard on the tires."

"We're acquainted with that," the old man replied.

It was hard on the car, too, said Mr. Simpson, and he would like to make him an offer. He liked old cars. He liked to save them from the hazards of the open road. This fine old car, which still seemed to run, should be taken off the road before it was ruined. He would give Floyd Warner $1,500 for the car, just as it was, and pay the trucking costs to get it back to his home in Long Beach. He wanted to know what Floyd Warner thought of an offer like that? Uncle Floyd said he thought it a reasonable offer for a car that burned oil, and was now burning rubber, but over thirty-six years he'd got accustomed to it and saw no reason why he should give it up.

"Make it two grand," Mr. Simpson said, "which will buy you something a little bigger. How about a Buick? How about a late model Olds?"

If he could believe what he'd heard, Uncle Floyd said, all the late model cars weren't built to give service. The Maxwell had given him no trouble to speak of, outside of a little oil.

"Make it an outright sale of three thousand dollars!" said Mr. Simpson. If he didn't want another car he needn't buy it. He and the boy could take a train, or the plane.

"I was offered six thousand dollars," Uncle Floyd lied, "even back before I put the new rubber on it. With the new rubber on it I feel obligated to wear it out."

"My offer stands on the car alone," said Mr. Simpson. "I've no need of the antique that comes along with it."

Uncle Floyd said, "Mr. Simpson, what would you say is the yearly fall of snow in Long Beach?"

Mr. Simpson could see he was crazy. "If it snowed in Long Beach, Mr. Warner, you think Mrs. Simpson and I would live there?"

"That I don't," said Uncle Floyd, and took the boy for a walk to take the kink out of their legs.

They were three days crossing Utah, part of it because the boy took the wrong turn on the freeway and they were forty miles north, almost to Ogden, before he realized what had happened. Floyd Warner did not realize it at all, because he was riding in the trailer, sleeping. There was a law against that, but if anything happened the boy would say the old man had been taken sick—and that was how he looked. The boy thought he might have caught something from the sheep, or overexerted himself. If he didn't feel too well, and he didn't, he would go without eating until he felt better. That was how he got the "poisons" out of his system. If everybody would do that, in his opinion, eighty percent of the doctors would go out of business, and the remaining twenty percent would take care of women's backaches. Every woman in the world, including Aunt Viola, had an ache in her back.

In the mountains east of Salt Lake it got cold at night, and the wind rocked the trailer. The only food the old man would touch was hot water, with canned milk in it. It's a shame to say so, but riding up front, alone, the boy was afraid. He stared up the road hoping he would see the smiling face of the girl, waving to him. There was room in the cab for two more people, now that he was alone. When he stopped to see how the old man was doing, he looked dead. He didn't snore. He just lay out on his back, with his mouth open. But he always had strength enough to shout at him to close the door. The cold mountain weather seemed to suit him, however, and he was up the next morning for an early breakfast. According to the map he spread out on the counter they now had less than seven hundred miles to go. But they were only going about two hundred miles a day. The town of Chapman, where Viola was buried, appeared to be near the middle of the Platte River, but the old man assured him that was a mistake on the map. The town set to the north. The river itself was a mile away. You could tell it by the willows that grew along it and the quicksand that would swallow up horses and wagons. Floyd Warner had sunk in it to his waist when he had been a boy.

Being anxious to get there, and feeling better, his Uncle Floyd took the wheel. They had a strong tailwind that wagged the trailer, but it pushed the car right along with it, saving gas. In country so empty everything looked small, the mile-long freight trains were like toys, and people along the highway crouched on their bags to get out of the wind. A fine powdery dust settled on the boy's lips, and mixed with his gum. He was just sitting there, not driving, when he saw the girl with her long hair blowing, looking half frozen, but with the big warm smile on her face.

"That's them!" he cried. The young man was crouched off the road, out of the wind. It might have been because the girl had hardly any clothes on, her arms clasped tight to keep her shawl from blowing, or it might have been just seeing her so often, always smiling, as if she knew them, but whatever it was the old man stopped the car. The girl didn't seem to believe it. Maybe it was hard to tell, they went by so slow, that they had actually stopped. She just stood there, watching, while the young man came running toward them, swinging his pack. He came up on the boy's side of the car, and put his head in the window he had run down for him. Was it the blackness of his beard that made his lips so red? Seeing him so close like that, and so clearly, the boy knew why he looked so familiar. He was the Lord Jesus of the jigsaw puzzle sent to him by Aunt Viola, with the eyes that were said to follow you wherever you went. But they didn't have to follow anybody who was trapped right there in the car.

"Far out, Dad," he said, looking them up and down. "Where you people headed?"

The Dad bit caught the old man off guard. "Up a ways," he came back. "Where you headed, boy?"

"Ohio," he replied. "Have a job in Ohio."

"Wouldn't it pay you to take a bus and get there?"

That caught the young man off *his* guard. "It's not much of a paying job," he said, "just a job."

"We've got no room in the cab, boy." His Uncle peered around as if he might find some. So did the young man.

"Far out!" he said. "Really far out."

"How's that, boy?"

"Far out, Dad," he replied, "a real gasser."

Did he mean the car, the old man at the wheel, or the whole kit and kaboodle? The boy did not speak this language but he understood it was complimentary. Before the old man replied the young one withdrew his head to make room for the girl, with her wide,

97

white smile. Tangled strands of her hair crisscrossed her face. "Hi!" she said.

"Hi!" the boy echoed.

"We've been expecting you," she said. *"Honest!"*

The boy said, "We had to stop. We had to stop and buy tires. We wear tires out fast because of the trailer."

The old man said, "Shut up a bit, will you? That's more than he's talked since we left California."

"We're from California, too," she said.

"I was just telling your friend"—the old man did not look at him—"we've got no room here in the cab. For one maybe, not two."

The young man said, "We could ride in the trailer."

The boy sat silent, his eyes down the road. Was the old man going to say there was a law against it, after he had ridden in it himself?

"There's a law, you know," he said—the girl seemed to know that, her head wagged—"but I can't leave you out here, with night coming on. I suppose we can take you where you can find shelter."

"Find shelter?" said the young man. "That's a gas!"

"Boy," said the old man, "what are you saying?"

"He means that's just wonderful! He really does, don't you?"

The young man had walked back to get in the trailer. Uncle Floyd yelled at him, "Hey, hold on there!" and shut the motor off to go back and check on him. The door to the trailer had to be locked to make sure it wouldn't fly open. His Uncle unlocked it, then stepped inside to see what was lying around that somebody might swipe. There was quite a bit.

The young man said, "Why don't you let me drive, Dad, and you ride back here."

"God-a-mighty, boy, you got a nerve!"

"We can't run away with you in it, Dad," he said, "and the kid up front." When he said *kid*, the girl tilted her head to catch the glance of the boy: he lowered his eyes.

"Stanley's honest," said the girl, "I mean, he really is."

"His name's Stanley?" asked the old man. "What's yours?"

"Joy," she said. Her hair just naturally hung in strands over her face, and she had to keep parting it with her fingers. Her lips were so chapped the boy knew it must hurt her to smile.

"What I'm going to do," the old man said, "is let the boy ride back here with you. If that's all right with you."

"Is it all right with *you?*" the girl asked the boy.

"Oh, sure," he said.

"I know he'd welcome the chance," Uncle Floyd said, "to talk to somebody besides me." He stepped out of the trailer and let Stanley step in; he looked all around it, then sat down on the chair. The girl said, "Oh my, isn't it groovy?" and sat down on the bunk. The boy stood off to one side, in the kitchen. "Sit down, boy!" Uncle Floyd said, "or you'll fall down when she starts to wag." The boy sat down at the other end of the bunk from the girl.

"Now make sure you latch the door when I close it, you hear?" The boy knew how to do this, and got up to latch it. He sat himself down again, then waited forever for the car to start.

"Your old man a good driver?" Stanley asked.

"He's not my old man," the boy answered. "He's my next of kin."

Suddenly the dishes began to rattle, and the girl took a grip on the bunk post. "Fasten your seat belts," Stanley said, but she did not laugh. The boy had never ridden in the trailer when it was moving, and he didn't like it. He felt trapped. Stanley didn't seem to mind and took an orange from his pack and slowly peeled it, sniffing his fingers. He put the strips of peel in his jacket pocket, and divided the orange in three equal sections, offering one to the boy, who shook his head.

Stanley said, "Take it, kid," so he took it. It was better to sit and eat than do nothing. The wagging of the trailer was not so bad, but the rattle of the dishes and pans was deafening. How had the old man been able to sleep in it? He had been sick. The cars coming toward them now had their lights on but it was not dark in the trailer. The windows tilted upward and the sky behind them was bright. After a while the girl used paper towels to try and stop the dishes from rattling, and before she had finished Stanley pulled her down on his lap. "No," she said, but he held her. He put his right hand up under her dress into the top of the purple stocking she was wearing, his other hand took a grip on her hair at the back of her neck. In order not to see what they were doing the boy rolled over on his side, facing the wall, his head thumping on the side when the trailer jerked. The smell of the exhaust was strong on the grades when the motor pounded, and they were hardly moving, but on the down side it would blow out and the boy could smell the peel of the orange. But he was not feeling so good by the time they stopped. The lights of the gas station flooded the trailer and the girl stood up to look at her face in the mirror, using a paper towel to wipe around her mouth. When Stanley opened the door the old man was right there, peering in.

"You people all right?"

"We're gassed," said Stanley. "You ever been high on pollution?"

He stepped out to stretch his legs, followed by the girl, then the boy. Some real Indians were standing by a Coke machine looking at them. A freight train was passing through, the crossing bell clanging, and the racket was so bad the boy could not hear a word the old man said to Stanley, or what Stanley said to him, although he could see their lips moving. The girl followed Stanley out to the highway, where she turned and waved to the boy, then the two of them walked along the edge of the road into the town. The main street was all lit up, an arrow flashing downward above a diner, where five or six double trailer trucks were parked at the front. Most of the noise had left town with the caboose, the lights blinking up the grade to the west, but the old man didn't ask him, then or later, how he liked riding in the trailer, nor did he have much to say about it himself. On the menu in the diner he read that they were in Rawlins, a Great Place to Live.

Four

ALL NIGHT LONG trains rattled the dishes as if the trailer itself was moving, and the boy often had that impression when he peered through the window. The letters on the boxcars drifted one way, then another, but who was moving? Puffs of wind rocked the trailer as if they were tilting on a curve. How could Rawlins be a great place to live if nobody slept?

The old man did not get up till the trailer was warm inside from the sun. He asked the boy about the smell of the orange, and the boy explained. Apropos of nothing special the old man said that he'd been studying the map on the wall of the gas station, and there was a route, going south out of Rawlins, that went like an arrow right down to the Rockies, which he thought the boy, instead of just passing by, might like to see. Did he think the boy was so dumb he didn't see through something like *that?* Did he think they were going to duck them *that* way? On the other hand he did want to see the Rockies, and he also didn't want to seem ungrateful. With his own eyes, however, from the window of the diner he could see what must be snow on the Rockies, but his Uncle said he probably couldn't tell snow from clouds. He did take the trouble to ask in the station and the attendant said, "Mister, you kidding?" There *was* snow in the mountains, but he was mostly concerned with the rap he could hear in the motor. It was louder when the engine idled than when it pulled on a grade. He said a bearing like that might run for weeks, or it might wear a hole in the motor by evening. He recommended four quarts of his heaviest oil, and no higher cruising speed than twenty miles an hour. With one thing or another they didn't leave Rawlins until almost noon, taking it very easy, so they were going little more than twenty miles an hour when they approached the turnoff east of town. Both Joy and Stanley were seated on the guard-rail so you couldn't be sure they were hitchhiking or not. The girl waved to the boy, who could see that Stanley was hunched over playing his harmonica. About fifty yards down the road the old man stopped.

The girl was the first to reach the cab window, and put her big, friendly smile right into the boy's face. Just sitting there in the sun had made her smile whiter, and her nose red.

"Isn't it a groovy day!" she cried.

The boy said it sure was.

"You want to let them in the trailer?" the old man asked him, but he did not tell him to get in with them. They had to wait for the girl to go back and get Stanley since he hadn't even troubled to get up off the guardrail. He went on playing his mouth organ as if the boy wasn't there, holding the trailer door open, and the girl said, "You can lock it if you want to. We don't care." He didn't lock it, he just banged it shut and came back and got in the cab with his Uncle. After a while the old man said, "I don't like that smart-alecky boy." That was all. It was a groovy day just like the girl had said. They had a tail wind from the southwest so that they cruised along with no more pedal than if they were idling. In the midafternoon the old man got sleepy and they pulled over to the side to let the boy take the wheel. They both got out of the cab to stretch their legs. Even better than in Rawlins the boy could see the Rockies, like a row of white teeth on the horizon, with high thunderheads of cloud piling up to the east. On the flat bottom side of the clouds a veil of rain was falling, the purple color almost the same as the girl's hip-length stockings. He thought the view was something she shouldn't miss.

"Hey, you people," the old man said, and slapped his hand on the door of the trailer. Nothing happened. Had they fallen out or something worse? The old man slapped the door again, then pulled it open as if he thought they would step right out. The boy was the first to see the hairy ass of Stanley lying on the bunk, his pants wadded on the floor, and he first thought he was just sprawled there, taking a nap. Then he saw, behind, the white leg of the girl thrust straight up so that it touched the upper bunk, but the rest of her body, except for one brown arm, was sunken into the bunk that Stanley lay on top of, his face twisted toward them with a wide, grimacing smile. His Uncle Floyd had to put his head in to see clearly, and then it took him longer to figure it out. Didn't he believe it? The boy saw it all very clearly right off. Shrilly, the old man shouted, "What in the name of Jesuschrist are you doing?"

"Fucking," he replied, and went on with it.

The crash of the door broke the pane in the window, and most of it fell inside, like breaking glasses. The old man went around and got behind the wheel, forgetting that they had stopped to let the boy drive, then he had to lean over and run down the window to ask the boy if he meant to just stand there, or get back in the car. He got back in the car, and not far down the road that veil of purple rain he had seen near the mountains mostly proved to be hail that bounced like popcorn on the engine hood.

The boy got behind the wheel a little after midnight, and drove all night. When he stopped for gas he thought Joy and Stanley would get out and sneak off somewhere, the way *he* would, rather than wait for daylight and have to look the old man in the face. But they didn't eat, use the toilets, or anything else. The old man slept in the cab, and the boy saw him only when the car lights flashed through the windshield, his arms around the pillow that was tucked up under his chin. The strange thoughts he was having were largely due to the people riding in the trailer. He hadn't thought of it, as he did now, as a trailer with something in it. A cattle trailer. His father had one for horses and steers. They had been pulling such a trailer, with the boy's Hereford calves, the night of the accident near Palmdale, and he awakened to see the leaves burning in the pepper tree over the smoking wreck.

Just before sunrise he could see North Platte but he thought he would starve before they reached it. He parked the car across from an all-night diner, the long counter full of truck drivers. The boy sat in a booth, near the jukebox, while his Uncle went back to the men's room. The window reflected the counter, and the fluorescent lights, but if he put his face to it he could see out. The door to the trailer hung open, and the girl stood there, combing her hair. Stanley sat on the running board of the car, lacing his shoes. The boy was glad for them that it was still dark and they could sneak away without the old man seeing them. He watched them closely to see if Stanley tried to swipe something from the trailer. The girl closed the door, wrapping her shawl tight around her, but instead of walking off in the other direction they came across the parking lot toward the diner. Were they so hungry? How could they think about eating after something like that? They came in together, and knowing the boy was there somewhere the girl looked all around until she saw him, then she smiled and waved. Stanley gave her his pack, some change from his pocket, and she came toward the booth while he headed for the men's room.

"Whoever slammed the door broke the mirror," she said. "Now we've got no mirror." She sat across from him, smiling. "Your eyes are red. Didn't you sleep?"

"I drove almost all night."

"You should smile more," she said, and smiled at him. "It's being together that matters. Don't you know that?"

By being together did she mean what he thought she meant? Smiling, she tipped her head to one side, like a bird, and sang

"Come to-gethhhhhh-ur"

clapping her hands softly. Did it lead him to smile?

"That's better," she said, "don't be such a sourpuss."

Stanley came from the men's room and sat down beside her, his beard speckled with paper towel lint.

"Where's the old man?" Stanley asked him. "Throwing up?"

"He's not sick," he replied. "He's just pooped."

"He's sick, too, kid," said Stanley. "All the nonfuckers are sick. Maybe you're sick, too."

"He's not sick," said the girl. "He's just been driving all night."

The boy was not stupid, but he was still less than twelve and this sort of discussion made his eyes smart and water. He could hardly see the old man coming down the aisle toward them, rubbing at his glasses with a piece of paper towel. Without his glasses he didn't see, until too late, who the boy was sitting there in the booth with. He did not sit down. There was towel lint on his glasses when he put them to his eyes.

"Breakfast is on us," said the girl, looking at Stanley. "It really is, isn't it?"

"Far out, Pop," he said. "All you can eat."

Uncle Floyd just stood there in the aisle, winding his watch.

"Sit down, Dad," said Stanley, but the boy knew he would not sit down, and dimly understood why. It was not because of Stanley, or because of the girl, or even whatever it was they had been doing, but that the three of them were now seated together in the booth. They were all young, and he was old. They were on the one side, and he was on the other. The boy knew that on the instant. He knew it better than anything else.

The old man said, "What do you people do? Besides, that is."

"Very funny," said Stanley. "A real gasser."

"He's a Weatherman," said Joy, "aren't you, darling?"

"You're a what? said the old man. "Where'd you learn it?"

"I picked it up the hard way, Pop."

"I suppose they teach that in the schools now, don't they?"

"They teach everything in the schools now," said Stanley. Joy smiled.

"This what you plan to do in Ohio?" asked the old man.

"I've a big job waiting for me," said Stanley. "A real big job."

"I'm starved!" said Joy. "Isn't everybody starved?"

She turned to look at the menu on the wall behind the counter. "I want a dozen eggs, a pound of bacon, a bowl of oatmeal, and prunes, and three orders of toast."

Uncle Floyd checked his watch against the clock on the wall, then he said, "You got fifteen minutes till the bus leaves," and walked off.

"Uncle Floyd," the boy cried, "you didn't eat!"

At the door he stopped as if to think that over. "I lost my appetite, boy," he said, and walked out the door.

"He don't like to watch us eat. He don't like to watch us—" The girl placed her hand over Stanley's mouth, then yelped when he bit her finger. All the men at the counter turned to stare at them, the girl sucking her finger, the boy with his face pressed to the window where the reflection revealed it was just the three of them against all the rest.

Book Three

Book Three

One

- -

IN NORTH PLATTE, NEBRASKA, at six-thirty in the morning, in a diner with people who urged him to do it, the boy had the first hot cup of coffee in his life. He liked it better with two extra spoonfuls of sugar, and more cream. When they came out to the car they found the old man asleep in the trailer, in the boy's upper bunk. He lay facing the wall, and didn't move when the girl covered him with a blanket.

"Why don't I drive?" said Stanley, so he drove and the boy sat on the seat near the window, the girl in the middle. A hazy overcast sky kept the morning sun out of their eyes. The girl sang songs the boy had never heard, clapping her hands. People who tried to sing without a piano or something embarrassed him. You couldn't see it on the road, but all across Nebraska the road was downgrade, and easy on the motor. Except for her singing, he liked riding along with them in the cab. "I knew he wasn't your old man," said Stanley. "You know how I knew?" The boy didn't. "If he was your old man, and worth a shit, he wouldn't have asked you to get back in the trailer with us. We could have dumped you. We could have dumped the two of you. He was more interested in what he thought we might swipe than he was in you."

The girl said, "Oh, Stanley!"

"It's time he figured out who his real friends are," Stanley said. "It's not some old fart."

"You like your Uncle?" the girl asked.

The boy pumped his head up and down. He pressed his lips together to keep them from trembling.

"You're still a kid," said Stanley, "and that's kid stuff. When you grow up you'll see it different."

The girl sang

> *"You never give me your money*
> *You only give me your fun-ny pa-per*
> *And in the middle of negotiations*
> *You break down"*

which made no sense at all. He wondered what they would all do when they reached Chapman, and how long it would be before someone picked them up.

Would he miss them? Would he never see them again? On a sign in Grand Island he saw the name CHAPMAN and yelled, "That's it!" and pointed at it.

"Half an hour," said Stanley. "Just in time for lunch."

"Your people live there?" asked the girl.

"She died," said the boy.

"You don't know it," said Stanley, "but you're lucky. I had to fight 'em. All *you* got to do is let them die off."

A few miles out, the boy could see the elevator, with a grove of barren trees to the left of the tracks; along the highway there was nothing but a gas pump in front of a false-front store.

"Oh, look!" cried the girl. Off where she pointed, in the direction of the river, gravestones shimmered in the high noon light. Rows and rows of them. Did that explain the emptiness of the town?

"They're all buried there," the boy said firmly.

"Oh, it's lovely!" cried the girl. "I want to see it!"

A smooth dirt road led off the highway toward it, and far down at the road's end they could see the willows. "That's the river," he said with assurance, just as if he knew. A quarter mile or so south they turned to the left, then to the right at the cemetery entrance. Trees grew high around it on three sides, and the grass on the graves had recently been cut. An old hand pump with an enameled dipper attached to the nozzle stood near the gate.

Stanley said, "I'm thirsty, but not *that* thirsty."

"Can *anybody* be buried here?" she asked.

"You got to be dead first," said Stanley.

"Don't be stupid," she said, and left the car to run to the gate, where she kicked off her sandals, then she ran between the rows of stones flapping her arms like wings, her shawl trailing out behind her like the tail of a kite.

"Somebody see you they'll put you in the nut house!" yelled Stanley. He stopped at the pump and worked the handle. Nothing happened.

"First you've got to prime it," said the boy, who knew about pumps.

"What you mean, prime it?"

"You put water in at the top, then pump it."

"If you've got water, why bother?" said Stanley. He bothered, however, taking the canvas water bag from where it was squeezed between the hood and the fender. There was still water in it, and the boy poured it in at the top while Stanley pumped. The rising sound of the water was like that of an animal being sick. Stanley raised the dipper, took a taste of the water, and spit it out. The boy did it the way he had learned from his father, by cupping his hand over the nozzle then pumping the handle until the water had backed up in the pump. Bending over he drank what didn't splash in his face. The girl had stopped running up and down between the stones, and stood leaning on one, her foot turned up so she could look at its bottom.

"Ohhhhhhhhhh—" she cried.

"You have to put on an act!" Stanley yelled at her.

She did not reply. She let herself sag down on the mound of a grave so she could pull up her foot and look at it closely. Her long hair was the color of the grass that grew tall as hay at the edge of the clearing, or in yellow tufts close to the stones, out of reach of the mower. When she did not reply Stanley picked up her sandals and walked between the stones toward her, reading off the names. "Hofer, Seidel, Manson, Klinger, Cook—"

"What Seidel is that, boy?"

Stanley turned from the stones to see the old man, hatless, with his hands cupped to the pump nozzle. The boy was pumping. He thought it made a lot of noise for a cemetery pump.

"Lyle C.," replied Stanley, reading it off the stone.

"And which one of the Cooks?"

"Esther."

Both Stanley and the boy waited for him to say something. Uncle Floyd cupped the cold water to his face, then shook his head like a dog, his skin shining like leather. In the flat noon light he seemed to have no hair at all.

"Sewell, Wells, Horde, Youngblood—" Stanley chanted, then he stopped and shouted, "Where are the Jews, Dad? Don't they bury the Jews?"

"One of the Hordes married a Jew," he replied. "Forget his name." He thought a moment, added, "They went to live in Grand Island." He stooped for the hat he had dropped in the grass, then walked to stand in the road behind the trailer. The boy hadn't thought of him being bandy-legged, but he was. With a wet brown hand he shaded his eyes and looked across a field of corn stubble toward Chapman. With all of them here in the cemetery, what was there left to see? One grain elevator, two or three houses, a barn with a MAIL POUCH sign on the roof, all of it in what might have been a grove in the summer but the trees were now either dead or leafless. The old man in the road would see what he remembered, but the boy's squinting eyes saw only what was there. He didn't think it much.

"You hear that?" Stanley yelled to the girl. "One ran off with a Jew. Pretty lucky, right?"

The girl didn't seem to hear him. She crouched almost bent double, with one leg pulled up and the foot twisted around so she could look at its bottom.

"That's it, boy!" said the old man, and wagged his

finger at a two-story house with a run-around porch. At the upper-floor windows the green shades were drawn. A lightning rod topped the roof. The grass had not been cut, as in the cemetery, and it grew hay-high along the sides of the house, giving the impression that the porch was sinking into the ground. The barn with the MAIL POUCH sign set so far behind it the boy wasn't sure that it went with the house. Uncle Floyd put his hat on his head, said, "She sat there for fifty years looking over here, and now she can lie here forever and look over there. If you feel a pair of eyes on you, boy, that's sure to be her grave."

This cemetery had looked small to the boy from the road, but it contained a lot of stones. Some were too old and weathered for either of them to read, others were so new they looked like samples. The boy found Aunt Viola, not because he felt her eyes, but her stone was so new it looked plastic. There had not been room for her with the others, but Uncle Floyd pointed out she would have cooler summers with more shade. It embarrassed the boy to see the stone was so small. Viola Warner had lived twelve years less than a century and he felt that her stone should look like it. His impression was that she must be small and almost brand new. The sod cut to dig her grave had been put back on it like strips of carpet. The crumpled tinfoil had peeled away from the coffee can with its withered flowers. His Uncle Floyd stooped to take the flowers from the can, toss them aside, then sprinkle what was left of the water on the grave. It disappeared without a trace, and the boy was certain he could hear it dripping on the lid of the casket. Every time it rained it would drip and ping, drip and ping. . . .

"Your mother's here somewhere," the old man said, and wheeled slowly as if he might see her. The boy didn't want to. For *his* mother to be here was all a mistake. What was right for Aunt Viola, with her great faith, was not right at all for his cheerful, foolish mother, with her Bible on the shelf with the cookbooks, a file for the candy recipes she had collected. If his mother's eyes were actually on him they were checking his ears and neck. Uncle Floyd was not strong in that department, and for a week now the boy had drunk a lot of water, but not washed with it.

Cries like the shrieks of birds led him to turn and look toward the bearded Stanley, seated on a grave. The girl was sprawled face down across his lap. He had her skirt pulled up and her panties pulled down as if he intended to give her a spanking. Before she got it, sensibly, she shrieked. Her dirty bare feet wagged in the air, and when the boy got closer, and saw better, he noted the prickly red spots on her creamy white bottom. Stanley was using the point of his hunting knife to fish for the burrs. They were all over the soles of her feet as well, but first he had to get them out of her bottom. Several clusters of the sandburs were stuck like ornaments to her mini-skirt. The boy knew from experience that when you pulled a burr off, nine times out of ten you didn't get the prickly thorn. It had to be found before it was sat on, or it might disappear. Another thing he knew from personal experience was that you could *feel* them better than you could see them, but he was not in a position to be of much help.

Coming up behind him the old man shouted, "What in the God-a-mighty hell are you up to now?" Couldn't he see?

"She's got her ass full of burrs," replied Stanley. "What do you think?"

The girl made little yelps when he jabbed her, and her toes curled inward like fingers. The boy thought he might lend a hand with her feet, his eyes being very good for small splinters.

"Kid," said Stanley, without looking up. "You people got some mercurochrome or something?"

Yes, they did have something. The boy went off on the double, collecting burrs on his pants, to the tin of Band-Aids in the cabinet drawer. Stuck in with the Band-Aids was a bottle with skull and crossbones on the label. That meant it would sting, and anything that stung would do you good. He galloped back, passing the old man, who had stopped to pump his hat full of water, his face dipped into it for a drink.

"She can do her own goddam feet," said Stanley, making big red spots out of the small ones, "but first I've got to get them out of her ass." The boy hated to agree, but he could see the logic of it. Nor had the sting gone out of the treatment, from the way she yelled.

When Stanley had done what he could—he planned to do more later—he had to carry her piggyback to the trailer since she couldn't walk. The prickly itching was so bad she just sprawled out on her face and bawled.

"You're like a bunch of goddam kids!" Uncle Floyd yelled. "When the hell you expect to grow up?"

"Up where?" replied Stanley. He would have peered at the sky but the old man slammed the door in his face. They drove back into town on the road they had come out on, then along the highway to the Texaco pump in front of BELLE'S CAFÉ. Three or four old cars and two pickup trucks were parked at the side. A short gray-haired man, not so old as Uncle Floyd, came to the screen. Before he could speak he had to swallow the food in his mouth. Turning away, he said, "Emma, look at this!"

A gray-haired woman in a blue polka dot apron, her hair in curlers under a hairnet, came to the screen. She held a wad of apron squeezed in one hand, but what she saw didn't impress her. The boy was sorry she couldn't see the California plate on the rear.

"You people want gas?" said the old man.

Inside the café a voice said, "What'd he want gas for? That burn gas?" Then he guffawed.

"I'm Floyd Warner," Uncle Floyd said. "Would you be the one to have the key to the house?"

"We got one key, Mr. Warner," she said. "There's a lawyer in Grand Island with the other."

"Guess one key is enough, if it works," said Uncle Floyd.

Inside the café the same man guffawed. "He bring that wreck back for the auction, too?"

Everyone in the café had stopped eating to listen. The boy could hear them laugh.

"You'll find it pretty much the way she left it, Mr. Warner. Anybody will tell you that's how she liked it. Is that your boy?"

"We're related."

The woman gathered up a wad of the apron and squeezed it. "You plan to have an auction soon?" she asked.

"Let him get settled first, will you, Emma?"

"She's got a regular store of things, Mr. Warner. If the kids didn't want it, they left it to Viola. There's a lot they didn't want."

"There's always people to buy what you don't need," said the man.

"I wouldn't have thought that," said Uncle Floyd. "Where are they?"

"They're not all dead, if that's what you're thinking. We get two, three hundred people for a good auction."

From the broken window in the door of the trailer comes a sound like somebody gagging.

"Kids," said the old man.

The woman nodded her head. "You're going to need more room." To the man she said, "Key is in the cash drawer," and he left the screen to get it. The boy could hear the bell ring when the door banged open, again when it shut. He came back with a long, lead-colored door key on a paper clip, with a tab attached. The woman took it, said, "It's to the rear door. I suppose you know that. Nobody's used the front door since Mr. Warner."

"Him and God," said the old man.

The woman wasn't sure she had heard that right. Before she replied there was a racket in the trailer that sounded like scuffling. The voice yelled, "Stanley *don't!* Stan-ley DON'T!" The old man ran down the window on the driver's side and slapped his hand like a board on the car door.

"Quiet, goddam it!" he hollered. "You kids hear me?"

It was quiet, inside and out.

The woman said, "How many you got?"

"Three in all."

"You're going to need more room than you'll find," said the woman, and gave the boy the key.

"We'll look around, ma'am," Uncle Floyd replied, but when he let out the clutch it was so loose they just sat there, giving off smoke. Then it caught, and they swung around to head west, the old man waving at the faces crowding the screen door. The trailer rocked so bad crossing the tracks the boy could hear the dishes in the cabinet rattle. "That hasn't changed much either," the old man said, but mostly to himself.

Two

ON THE NORTH SIDE of the tracks basements had been
excavated for two stores that hadn't gone up. One
was full of cans and the bodies of wrecked cars. In
the weeds back from the road a cement sidewalk ran
from one vacant corner to the next vacant corner,
spears of grass shooting up between the slabs. Over
one corner a street lamp, the once milk-white globe
marked with overlapping rings of mudballs that had
stuck for a while, then dropped off. Far to the back
of a grove of trees the boy could see a chain swing and
two teeter-totters, indicating it had once been a park.
Aunt Viola's place, the house with two floors and the
green blinds drawn at the upper windows, sat in a
clearing of knee-high grass with a windbreak of ever-

greens at the back. Even above the ping of the motor he could hear cawing crows. A driveway went between hedges back toward the barn, but they had not been clipped for so long the room between them was narrow as a cow path, the branches dragging on the car and sweeping the trailer. Between the barn and the house there was no visible path. The one people still used came in from the side and led to a small white house across the street where chickens scratched in the side yard. A lawn swing tilted on its side in the front.

Uncle Floyd slapped his hand on the trailer. "We're stopping here. You people better move on."

"On what?" came the reply. "She can't sit or walk."

They could hear Joy moaning.

Uncle Floyd did not open the door to check. "Come along, boy," he said, and they waded through the high yellow weeds toward the house. The rear porch was screened in, but except where it was patched, with new pieces of screen, the boy could not see through it. The screen door had a thread spool for a knob, a hole kicked in the screen at the bottom. Chickens had wandered in and out, leaving their feathers stuck to the wire. "How she ever managed without a man," the old man said, "I'll never know." He opened the screen and they stepped in on the porch. Along the house wall, blocking the window, were four or five golden oak iceboxes, of assorted sizes, topped off with milk pails, enamel water pails, and a high pile of straw hats. Back in the corner, their tops hooded with flour sacks, were machines that the boy had never seen. They appealed to him, however, because they had cranks, and were good for something.

Aloud the old man asked, "Now who'd want a cream separator?"

There were also bushel baskets of pots and pans, and a brass boiler, with its lid. The boy still had the brains he was born with and said, "If they're antiques, Uncle Floyd, they're worth money."

"Quiet, boy," he replied, and unlocked the house door. They were in the kitchen, a room flooded with light from the window without curtains or a blind. Along one wall sat the stove, a kitchen range with the wire handle thrust up from one of the stove plates. Otherwise the top was clear of everything but burned matches. Someone had used the stove to scratch matches on it, and nothing else. The scratches made a crisscross hatching on the plates that turned from soot color to sulfur. All of the matches had burned down and died before the end. Before he said a word the old man's head began to pump, priming up his curses.

"Jesus H. Christ God-a-mighty!" he swore, and used the plate lifter to bang on the stove. The boy listened to him curse and saw what else there was to see. A round coal oil stove, with a wire handle, was topped by a large enamel teakettle, with oil-smoked sides. On the table that sat against the wall in the corner dishes and glasses were stacked to the boy's shoulders. He had never seen so many, even in a store, or glasses of so many colors. At the back, in a pile, were lampshades, and on the top of the shades a woman's hat with feathers. When the old man was quiet the boy could hear mice running in the walls. Besides that there were chairs, stacked with their legs up, and two kitchen cabinets, back to back, so you could use either one or the other, two or three ironing boards, and a carton full of iron handles, irons, and iron wax.

The door out of the kitchen was on a swinging hinge. The old man gave it a push and said, "That's new. When did she do that?" He pushed it inward to where it caught on a rug. The light through this door seemed to be all there was in the room behind it. The shade drawn at the window reflected the light back onto the bed, one end of it stacked with pillows. An afghan spread was turned back on wrinkled sheets. Aloud, as if he expected an answer, the old man asked, "Does it have to be so goddam dark?"

The boy said, "Aren't there any lights?" and looked for the switch on the wall. There was no switch, but on the table at the bedside stood a lamp, with a green shade, a wick curled in the bowl of clear oil. Uncle Floyd kicked the door, opening it wider, then stomped in to throw up the blind at the window opening out on the porch. That did little good because it was blocked by the iceboxes. The room smelled of burned lamp wick, coal oil, and the odor the boy associated with his mother's clothes closet, at once sweet and sour. On the floor was a saucer of soured milk, the edges nibbled by mice. A shoebox full of postcard pictures of cats, kittens, and puppies, along with postcards and letters, sat on the shelf below the lamp. The boy recognized the last letter, with the Smokey the Bear stamp, as his own. On the table at the foot of the bed, where they could be reached through the iron frame, soiled towels and dishcloths were piled in a washbowl, held down by a plate dirty with food smears. At the side a comb is stuck into the bristles of a brush with a silver back, and a small oval picture in a frame stamped with colored flowers. The picture showed a bearded man, seated erect on a chair, with a child on his knee holding a bird cage. The boy moved closer to see if the cage held a bird, but it is empty and the door is open. A woman stands behind him, one white hand resting on his shoulder, her hair parted and gathered in a bun at the neck. The white lace at her front is like the wings of a butterfly. The man's face is clear, his gaze directly forward, but the woman's eyes are so pale they look filmed. The boy thinks she looks frail and very young.

"Hand me that, boy," Uncle Floyd said, and turned so that the light fell on the picture. "That's him. That's the old bastard."

"Did the cage have a bird?" the boy asked.

"If it did, it's the only thing that ever got away!" Then he added, "That's either Viola or me, I don't know which."

The boy's gaze has moved to a case on the bureau behind him. It has a faded velvet lining, the color of dust, and in the clip of the lid there is the ivory frame of a mirror without glass. When he touches the lid the frame rattles. In the bottom of the case, in the velvet pockets where there had once been other objects, he sees three large bullets with dull brass casings and the ivory handle of a shaving brush. All but a whisk of the bristles are worn away.

This had once been the dining room, and the round oak table is now backed into the corner behind the door. The top of it is littered with pillboxes, medicine bottles (some of them with the skull and crossbones on the label), a lamp with a broken chimney, the wick in an empty bowl, glass salt and pepper shakers, cases for glasses, a cigar box without a lid, full of pins and bone hairpins, a cigar box with the lid made into a pin cushion, stuck full of threaded needles, hatpins, and a lady's cameo. There is a ball of tinfoil, a pocket watch with a chain, a flashlight, a pocket knife with a broken bone handle, two bed casters, a shaving strop, and a shoebox lid full of black and red checkers. There is more, but it would take all day to sort it out. What would an old lady want with a man's long-handled razor, a box of shotgun shells? He turns away to see the old man trying to pry open the folding doors. One is stuck. He curses it, kicking at it with his boot heel. One of the doors slides back so they can squeeze through into the parlor. A big coke burner with smoked glassine windows sits on a fireboard with the floral pattern worn away at the front and two sides. The fender of the stove shines like a bumper where somebody recently has sat on it. The nickel-plated ornament on the top has been pushed to one side to expose the fire lid, which is covered with half-burned matches like the kitchen range.

"Who in the goddam hell did that!" Uncle Floyd cried. He swept the burned matches off the top with his hand, then looked at the smear of soot and dust on the heel. "Who the hell do they take me for!" he cried, and the boy wonders what he means by that. There is a space around the stove, as if it might get hot, then the room is jammed with bureaus, chairs, and sideboards. The boy sees his reflection in half a dozen mirrors. At the large front window there are glass curtains that he sees like webs on the drawn yellow blind. In a corner near the door, where light falls on it, a three-legged table is covered with framed pictures. Maybe a dozen of them, with the larger ones at the back. Above it, as if through a window, a wild-eyed white horse with a flowing mane has been frightened by two yellow bolts of lightning, and rushes forward as if to leap into the room. The door itself has a center of beveled glass, the oval rim frosted to show off the engraving, and there are three panes of red, blue, and yellow church glass at the top. Perhaps they explain the curious color of the light in the room. Most of that color can be seen on the stairs where the red glows as if the carpet were burning, and the boy can see motes of dust sparkling in each beam of light.

"Wait here, boy," the old man said, and as he walked up the stairs the dust rose in a cloud at his feet. The boy hears his feet stomp the ceiling above him, then go from room to room, the doors creaking. In one room he stands: the silence of the house is like a tomb. The boy would leave, but his limbs will not move. He is able to gaze, with parted lips, at the two yellowed pages of sheet music on the rack of the black upright piano. A hymn book. The title of the hymn is "Crossing the Bar." One thing the boy has never learned is how to read music, and he wonders how this hymn sounds. His Aunt Viola loved music. He understood that she played as long as she could. A cushion had been placed on the piano bench, the lid of which would not quite close on the music. There were also pictures on top of the piano, but all he could see were the reflections of the window, where a fly buzzed behind the yellow blind. When the fly stopped buzzing he cried, "Uncle Floyd!"

No answer.

Fearing to look behind him, he went forward yelling, "Uncle Floyd! Uncle Floyd!" as he went up the stairs. At the top of the stairs the door ahead of him stood open, jammed with boxes and barrels like an attic. He could see little more than their outline against the dim light. The closed door he ignored, and came back to the front where the corner room looked empty. No rug on the floor, no clutter of objects, just a rocker facing the open window where the blind was half raised. Floyd Warner sat there, or rather he sagged there, his hands hanging limply between his knees, his head tilted as if to catch small sounds from the yard. Below the window the knee-high grass was like a field of grain. Beyond it the road they had just come down, leading across the tracks to the highway, and farther beyond, framed in the trees, the gleaming stones of the cemetery, the air smoking with the sprinklers that someone had turned on. The boy saw it plainly enough, but he doubted that the old man could see it. Had he fallen asleep? He was accustomed to an afternoon nap.

"Uncle Floyd," the boy said, but remained standing in the door. The green blind softened the light, and with nothing in the room to block it or absorb it the boy felt its presence. Within it, captive, he saw the figure seated on the narrow-backed armless rocker, both the seat and the back covered with pads made of patchwork quilting. Two dozen patches on the back side alone, in all shapes, colors, and materials. Everything left over had been put into it, as into this house. The old man who sat there did not impress the boy as his own great-uncle, Floyd Warner, but another object preserved from the past. Perhaps this corner room had been reserved for objects of that sort. Surely Aunt Viola had had something in mind when she cleared this room of all but the rocker, and came here, when she was able, to sit by herself. The boy really knew nothing about such matters and perhaps that proved to his advantage. He brought so little to what he saw, he saw what was there. This old man before him was not sleeping, since he sat in too strange a manner, his head up like a bird, rather than lolling on his front. "Uncle Floyd," he repeated, then he strained to control his terror as his legs ran on the stairs. He banged into things, he fell once, but he had only three doors to pass through and three rooms to cross. Out on the screened-in porch he shrieked, "Stanley! Stanley!" and saw that he was seated at the door to the trailer, examining the feet of the girl who lay on its floor. "Stanley!" he yelled, waving to him, and the young man stood up, taking the time to put the tail of his shirt into his pants, before he came at an easy lope toward the house.

"Uncle Floyd!" the boy cried. "He don't answer!"

"Maybe he's in the can."

"He's *not* in the can. There isn't any can. He's in a room upstairs. He doesn't answer."

"Cool it, kid. Maybe he just wants to be alone."

"He's sick, too."

"How you know he's sick?"

"He looks sick."

He let Stanley go ahead of him, one room then another, waiting while Stanley peered around, his head shaking, pronouncing the words "Far out, man," as they went up the stairs. The old man no longer sat there, perched like a bird, but had slouched to one side with the curled fingers of his right hand touching the floor. Stanley removed his hat to look at his face. "Hey, Pop," he said, "how you feel?"

What a question to ask a man who had died, the boy thought. Surely he could not be alive, and look as he did. Gray like putty, his jaw slack, but gleaming on his forehead was a film of moisture. Did the dead perspire like that? No, they did not. He was not dead, and when Stanley fanned his face with the hat his eyes opened. "Let's get you out in the air, Pop," Stanley said. "Air in here make anybody sick," then he started to lift him, but the old man shook him off.

"Boy," he said, "where you at?"

"Here, Uncle Floyd," he replied, and moved to where the old man could see him. He took a grip on the boy's arm, at the wrist—to take his hand would imply he was helpless—and pulled himself up. They stood there a moment while he got his bearings, his hand moving to the boy's shoulder.

"You going to stand here?" he said. The boy walked a half step ahead of him, slowly, down the stairs. He seemed to get a bit stronger crossing the kitchen, and as they stepped out on the porch he released the boy's shoulder, opened the screen himself.

"How you feel, Dad?" said Stanley. "You feel better?"

"I had a queasy spell," the old man said, breathing the fresh air, and went slowly ahead of them through the weeds toward the trailer. The girl was able to sit now, in the door of the trailer, with her right foot curled up so she could pick at its bottom. Her arch was so flat her foot was prickled all over, like a pin cushion.

"You poor darling," she said to Uncle Floyd. "Don't you feel good?"

"I feel as good as might be expected," he replied, "but I'm going to take a nap." She moved from the door to let him into the trailer, sprawl out on the bunk. His left leg hung down to the floor, and she leaned forward to slip the boot off. "Leave me alone!" he yelled.

"If the old fart wants to be left alone, leave him alone," said Stanley.

The boy said, "He'll be all right when he's rested."

"I'll either be all right or be dead."

"You mind we go sit on the porch?" Stanley asked the boy.

No, he didn't mind. Stanley crouched in the yard as if he meant to spring, and signaled to the girl to straddle his back, which she did. As they went off through the weeds she sang

> "*I never give you my number*
> *I only give you my situation*
> *And in the middle of investigation*
> *I break down.*"

"What is she saying?" the old man asked.

"It's a song," said the boy. "She's singing."

When the boy glanced in to see if that answer satisfied him his eyes were closed, and he looked asleep. The mournful sound he heard was the keening of the doves somewhere in the barn.

Three

In the late afternoon the boy sat at the door of the barn's loft. Like the house, it was crammed with all sorts of objects, some of it junk. A pile of horse collars, horse and buggy harness hung along the walls like decorations, corn shellers and grinders, a foot-treadle grindstone on which he sharpened the knife in his pocket, kegs of nails, a barrel of tar, tied-up bundles of asphalt shingles, cans of paint, brushes glued to the bottom of cans where the turpentine had evaporated, numberless shovels, hoes, and pitchforks, two unused rubber-tired wheels of a buggy, fly nets for the horses, and numerous machines supplied with cranks. They would all do something if cranked, but few would crank. In a box of articles he considered swiping the

wires and loose parts mystified him, all related to a
project he could no longer grasp. An oatmeal carton,
like the one in the trailer, wound a third of its length
with thin, covered wire, to which other wires, and
strange articles, were joined. In the bottom of this carton he found rocks that he understood to be crystals,
gleaming like mica, but to what use had they been put?
This collection he considered to be so valueless it
would never be missed. He put it to one side, along
with a doorbell that needed only a battery or something to ring it, and sat himself in the loft door, facing
the south. He had the same view as the window at the
front of the house, but it was wider and he saw more.
A train that had passed left a veil of smoke over the
town. He understood that a person might actually live
here, as well as die. All her long life his Aunt Viola,
troubled with her health but supported by her faith,
had lived on here while the others died and left to her
those things they valued. These things, many of them
useless, had survived. Into his pocket the boy had
slipped a coin found in the pocket of a coat, draped on
a doornail, that had survived all the people who had
spent or saved it since 1879. The meaning of this
escaped him in a manner he found satisfying. Already
he was old enough to gaze in wonder at life.

While he sat there he watched the old man ease himself out of the trailer and stretch his limbs. His hind-

quarters were cramped like an old dog's. Still bent over, his gait uncertain in the soft loam of the yard, he moved away from the trailer toward the corral adjoining the barn. As he walked his fingers fumbled at the buttons of his fly. The gate stood ajar, tilting inward, with a bucket upside down on one of the posts, the bottom of which he gave a slap as he passed. Patches of corn and grain, planted by cowpies, sprouted in the corral like a garden, the ground sloping away from the barn to the marshy tangle that drained the farm. The outside rail of the fence was almost lost in the weeds. All this long walk he had never stopped fumbling at the buttons of his fly, and they were open to his satisfaction by the time he reached the partial shade of a tree branch. His knees flexed, he pee'd down a stalk of stunted corn. When Uncle Floyd had been no older than the boy who now watched him from the barn loft window, had he watched another man pee in this manner, or was it something he had thought of himself, after milking the cows in the evening, or on his way to the barn after breakfast? A good pee in the open: not in the barn or the smelly, breath-catching stench of the privy. Was this one of the few things in the present that connected him to the past? He stood there, as a man will, with his gaze fastened on something or nothing, enjoying the great relief and pleasure it had been to pee. But he had also seen something. Almost at his feet, a step or two to the left; he bent his back, not his legs, to peer at it closer. Something on the ground. From where he sat the boy could not make it out. Curious, he called, "What you see, Uncle Floyd?" which naturally gave the old man a start.

"Where the hell you at?" he answered, peering around.

"Up here," called the boy, and waved, but he had turned back to what he had found. The boy used the ladder to come down from the loft, and the stable door to get into the corral. When he came up and stood beside the old man he saw nothing on the ground of interest. That was how well it was all one piece of the earth.

"A horseshoe?" he asked.

"An ox shoe, boy."

Whether or not it was an ox shoe (don't believe everything you hear, the old man had told him), this shoe was elevated above the level of the corral on a pedestal that was shoe shaped. The boy would have said the pedestal had been made for this particular shoe. It was an inch or so above the ground on the barn side, but at least two inches or more on the slope side. Two shoe nails firmly attached it to the pedestal.

"What pushed it up there?" the boy asked.

"Nothing pushed it up there," he replied. "It's the

earth that washed away from it. It's just where it always was. It's the earth that fell away."

The boy reflected on that for a moment. "You going to leave it?"

"What would we do with an ox shoe, boy?"

The boy was thinking they might nail it to the trailer for luck. They could use some luck. The old man said, "You like them, eh?"

Like who? The boy guessed his meaning only because he had turned to look toward the house. Now that the light had dimmed the flaking paint above the screened-in porch appeared to glow. The blue ball on the lightning rod blazed like a cold planet in orbit. But what held his eye was the warm glow behind the yellow blind at the window.

"You hear me, boy?" the old man asked.

Did he *like* them? He hardly knew. What he wondered was, did it matter?

"I'm glad it's you, boy," he said, "and not me. It goes against my nature, more than it does yours."

That took the boy by surprise. He had assumed it was the same nature they had, somewhat young in himself, somewhat old in his Uncle. How was he to know what this other nature might be?

"They've lit a lamp," the boy said, pointing toward the house, and the idea pleased him. It was the dark that made the house so spooky.

"They've what?"

"Lit a lamp," he repeated, and the old man strained to see it, squinting his eyes. "Them f—king goddam kids!" he swore, and went off toward the house. The boy couldn't see what was so bad about lighting a lamp. He tagged along behind the old man's trail through the weeds and saw him bang the screen door as he entered, then come back to grab the mop handle sticking out of a pail. As he moved closer he could hear the girl laughing; that was what he heard. Then he heard them talking, more than shouting, and two or three whacks like slapping a pillow. He crossed the screened-in porch into the kitchen, where the door to the room with the bed was half closed. Uncle Floyd stood behind it, the handle of the mop thumped it as he talked. The open half of the door framed the bureau mirror at the foot of Aunt Viola's bed, reflecting the glass shade and the smoking chimney of her lamp. The wick was up too high, causing it to smoke, and the boy could smell it on the draft through the door, along with the sweet scent he knew to be grass. The lamp glow was so bright he didn't at first see Stanley and the girl in the shadows to the side. They were sitting up, propped by pillows, side by side, in Aunt Viola's bed. Both of them were naked, but Stanley didn't look it with all that hair. His arms were folded, and he held the cigarette so that the heat of the lamp sucked the smoke under the shade, then out at the top. Of the girl, he sees mostly the top of her head, as she is bent over to peer at the bottom of her foot, her long yellow hair hanging around her like a screen.

"We don't dig it dark, Pop," said Stanley. "We're scared shitless of the dark, aren't we, baby?"

Maybe she lifted her head to speak to Stanley, her fingers combing her hair from her lips, but in the mirror she faces she sees the boy. "Hi, darling!" she said, and gave him a big smile. From where he stood the boy could not see the old man, but he could hear his wheezy, labored breathing: he saw the shadow of the mop head rise on the wall, then come down with a loud whack on the bed quilt. The girl began to laugh, and Stanley pulled up the quilt to cover them both. The boy could see they were hugging each other, laughing, when the head of the mop whacked them. All that it did was fill the air with a cloud of dust.

"You-you-you-you-YOU—" the old man yelled, building up with each *you* the boy's expectations, but all he ended up saying was "Blow out that lamp!" Whatever it was, he didn't want to see it. The two under the covers went on laughing. Did the old man do it? All of a sudden the room went dark. It went sooty black, with no more noise than the sound of clothes falling from a hanger. Muffled in the darkness the two of them went on giggling like kids.

"Uncle Floyd!" the boy yelled, but he was too scared to push the door wide open. The air smelled of what the two of them had been smoking, but on the draft he caught the whiff of something stronger burning. In the cave of darkness behind the bed, as if a match was struck, fire flickered. "Uncle Floyd!" he shrieked, "something's burrrr-ning!"

"I hope it's the two of them in hell. Serves 'em right!"

As if he had poured kerosene on it, the fire leaped up. The boy did not cry out: maybe the crackle of the flames recalled a terror better forgotten. He turned and ran, kicking a pail someone had half filled with water, then he was out on the porch, through the screen door with a thrust that almost unhinged it, and like a rabbit he cut through the weeds as if the fur on his back was burning. He passed the car and the trailer, then he entered the clearing of short grass approaching the barn, where he heard, like a timber splitting, the loud bang of the screen to the porch. That was the way the old man would slam the door to the trailer if the boy left it open. He did not look back, fearing he would see him, in his gleaming yellow hard hat, coming toward him. In the field on the left a startled cow lifted her head to watch him pass. On he went to where a wide ditch fenced the pasture, and he sank into it like feathers, the soft matted grass sweet smelling as hay. Insects droned above him, others crawled beneath him, and far behind him the confused sounds of commotion. Horns tooted. Near, then far, several dogs bayed. When he pushed himself up, eyes level with the ditch rim, the sky behind the barn was like one end of a rainbow. Black and white smoke billowed, and in the roiling cloud he saw tongues of flame like bolts of lightning. Stanley would like it. He would have liked a better view of it all himself. The tolling of a church bell made him think of Aunt Viola, and that her eyes would be on him right at this moment. What would she think? At least she would know he hadn't started the fire. The dying crackle of it now came to him faintly, and once he imagined he felt its heat. Anyone approaching would have seen the last of the glow in his eyes. Some of the trees along the driveway had taken fire and sent up showers of sparks, like fireworks. It was very much like Uncle Stambaugh's yarns about the Fourth of July. Then it all died away, like a sunset, and he was suddenly cold. A heaviness that was in neither his arms nor his legs, but like something he had swallowed, persuaded him to just lie there. Nobody came for him. Nobody hooted calling his name. He had once felt that he would surely die to be alone like that in the night and forgotten. But nothing happened. He felt nothing but the ants inside of his clothes. He might have lain there all night, just to show he could do it, if it hadn't been for the invisible cows, their movements like that of approaching monsters in a horror movie.

From the corner of the barn he could see the brick

chimney tilted like a ladder toward the wall that was missing. A fire still smoldered in the kitchen range and smoke came out of one length of the stovepipe, like a truck exhaust. Just a yard or two away—that was how it looked—the coke burner in the parlor glowed like a piece of charcoal. He thought it all looked small, as if the great heat had caused it to shrink. All around what was left the weeds had burned away but still smoked and flickered at the outer edges. There was very little rubble. The cream separators, once on the porch, had toppled in a pile like so many milk cans, but the blackened iron frame of the bed, where the two of them had lain, looked ready for making. The strong odor he smelled was that of hot metal and smoldering weeds.

Until he walked toward the fire, and had to move around the trailer, he hadn't noticed that the car was missing. The weeds that had swept the underside of the car were shiny with grease. Without the car to support it, the trailer tilted, and the coupling bolt was sunk into the yard as if someone had banged it with a hammer. The girl sat in the tilted trailer doorway, combing her hair. Behind her Stanley sprawled out on the lower bunk, smoking. Neither was surprised to see him.

"Where you been?" asked Stanley. "You missed a good fire."

He said, "Where's Uncle Floyd?" and peered around as if he might see him. Beyond the glow of the ashes, like dimmed car lights, were the faces of the people who had gathered to watch. They sat in their cars, or stood back under the trees, their eyes glowing like gems. The boy guessed that they had waited for the fire to cool in order to see what there was, if anything, behind it. None of them spoke or moved. They had probably expected to see more than they did.

Stanley said, "Too bad you missed it, man. It was a really good fire."

"Pay no attention to him," she said.

"You should ask *her* about fires," said Stanley. "She really digs fires."

"Where did he go?" the boy asked.

"Who knows?" replied Stanley. "Maybe up in smoke."

"Pay no attention to him," the girl repeated. Her hair, fanned out over her shoulders, appeared to have real lightning bugs trapped in it.

Stanley said, "He didn't care if we burned up or not. He took off without looking back. I watched him. You can see the way he took off in the way the trailer dropped."

She said, "It broke three cups and the percolator top."

"That was already broke."

"Not in *pieces*. There'll be no more *perk*-olator coffee."

Stanley asked, "Where you suppose he took off to?" The boy had no idea. Now that Aunt Viola had left them, what other place was there? "How about that place across the tracks?" said Stanley. "Maybe he wants to bury that car there."

"Pay no attention to him."

"What you plan to do?" said Stanley. "You can't stay here, man. What else is there to burn?"

"He's doing what we're doing," she said, "aren't you?"

Why didn't he ask what they were doing? Through the film forming on his eyes he seemed to see Stanley through rain-weighted branches.

"Don't look at me, kid. It's not my idea."

"Stop calling him *kid*," she said. "He's not a kid anymore, are you?"

Stanley got up from the bunk and spread his legs to step over the girl into the yard. At the edge of the smoking grass he unbuttoned his pants, pee'd on some of it. "What a tool!" he said. "First you start a fire with it, then you put it out." He turned back to the girl. "Which is sorer, your ass or your feet?"

"I'd rather sit," she replied.

"You two sit," he said, "while I walk over and get us some food." He walked around the smoking rubble where the house had been and they could see him out-lined against the firelit faces. Far back on the highway a neon sign flashed the word EAT.

"He just took off?" the boy asked.

The girl put up her hands like a magician who had just dissolved something into the air. The idea pleased her. She seemed to see it drifting away, like smoke.

"Why'd he leave the trailer?"

"For us, silly. Besides, where he's going, maybe he won't need it."

She raised her eyes from him to look at the sky behind the barn. Part of it was still glowing with the sunset, and the boy could see the branches of the trees against it. Two of the trees were so full of birds they looked like leaves. The racket they made was like the grackles back in Rubio. Had they gathered like the people to watch the fire?

"You know about birds?" she asked.

"What about them?"

"You know what *old* birds do when their time has come?"

No, he didn't. Was there anything of interest he actually knew?

"Well, when they are old, and their time has come, they just go off alone in the woods and die. That's why you never see any old dead birds, you realize that? There's just millions of birds and they have to die, sometime, but you never see a one of them unless they're hurt."

It amazed the boy to realize the truth of that, and shamed him to think that he hadn't known it.

"It's nature's way," she said, "and people should live according to nature. Some people really do." She stood up, suddenly. "You hear that?"

All he heard was the cooling crackle of the fire, like a piece of crumpled paper unfolding. Her eyes remained on the orange glow behind the barn. "That's the really big fire. You hear it?"

He stands before her, listening. Raising her long arms skyward she moans, "OOOOOoooooo MMMM-mmmmmmmmmm," then again, "OOOOOoooooo MM-MMMMmmmmmmmm!" He thinks it must be an animal call of some kind, or at least for birds. "Fire transforms," she pronounced. "You hear it in the fire."

He stands feeling the warmth of the one they had had on his back. She has tilted her head back to gaze at the sky, where the light on a plane's wing blinks like a planet. It reminds him of his Aunt Viola, and her faith. Already she is up there, somewhere, peering down. Soon now his Uncle Floyd would be up there, too, in spite of his mocking, stubborn will. The boy is relieved to feel that his eyes will be closed, not fastened on *him*. A man like his Uncle Floyd would not have the time for something trifling like that.

"The stars are balls of fire, too," she said, but gazing upward for so long has made her dizzy. The hand she had raised to shade her eyes she lowers to grip the boy's shoulder, ease the weight on her feet. With the other she seems to point to the corral, where the gate stands ajar. The boy feels a pleasurable chill of terror that someone stands there, beckoning to him. Would it be the old man, personally, or his ghost? "Look here, boy," it says, real as life, and points to the ox shoe that the earth has moved away from. There it sits, firmly nailed to its pedestal. He is glad to be reminded of the ox shoe, and plans to go and look for it in the light of the morning. It is in light like that that things are most easily found. In spite of all the eyes on him, and all the faith for him, he's going to need all the luck he can get. *They* are, that is. His Uncle would have been the first to tell them that. He is distracted by the girl's tightening grip on his shoulder in order to steady herself, stand on one leg, and by the glow from the fire examine the sole of her blackened foot.

"Fire purifies," she said, and gave him her big, warm, friendly smile.

71 72 73 74 75 8 7 6 5 4 3 2 1